Shane McBride was dangerous.

Of course, it wasn't his fault that she was wary of men—especially the alpha types. Or that what Christy craved right now was a peaceful life, a life dedicated to her new job and simple pleasures. A life rid of complications—especially the ones created by demanding men.

Besides, she hadn't been a bit interested when he'd taken off his shirt, she assured herself. The sight of his hard body hadn't doubled her pulse rate, either, and his heat hadn't sizzled through her fingertips, warming her from head to toe.

Yeah, right, she thought.

Dear Reader,

♪♫"Happy Birthday to us...."♪♫ Exactly twenty years ago this May, Silhouette Romance was born. Since then, we've grown as a company, and as a series that continues to offer the very best in contemporary category romance fiction. The icing on the cake is this month's amazing lineup:

International bestselling author Diana Palmer reprises her SOLDIERS OF FORTUNE miniseries with *Mercenary's Woman*. Sorely missed, Rita Rainville returns to Romance with the delightful story of a *Too Hard To Handle* rancher who turns out to be anything but.... Elizabeth August delivers the dramatic finale to ROYALLY WED. In *A Royal Mission*, rescuing kidnapped missing princess Victoria Rockford was easy for Lance Grayson. But falling in love wasn't part of the plan.

Marie Ferrarella charms us with a *Tall, Strong & Cool Under Fire* hero whose world turns topsy-turvy when an adorable moppet and her enticing mom venture into his fire station.... Julianna Morris's BRIDAL FEVER! rages on when *Hannah Gets a Husband*—her childhood friend who is a new dad. And in *Her Sister's Child*, a woman allies with her enemy. Don't miss this pulse-pounding romance by Lilian Darcy!

In June, we're featuring Dixie Browning and Phyllis Halldorson, and in coming months look for new miniseries from many of your favorite authors. It's an exciting year for Silhouette Books, and we invite you to join the celebration!

Happy reading!

Mary-Theresa Hussey

Mary-Theresa Hussey
Senior Editor

Please address questions and book requests to:
Silhouette Reader Service
U.S.: 3010 Walden Ave., P.O. Box 1325, Buffalo, NY 14269
Canadian: P.O. Box 609, Fort Erie, Ont. L2A 5X3

TOO HARD
TO HANDLE

Rita Rainville

Silhouette
ROMANCE™
Published by Silhouette Books
America's Publisher of Contemporary Romance

To my retreat buddies—
you know who you are.
Thanks for the love, laughter and support.

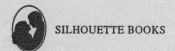

SILHOUETTE BOOKS

ISBN 0-373-19445-5

TOO HARD TO HANDLE

Copyright © 2000 by Rita Rainville

Visit Silhouette at www.eHarlequin.com

Printed in U.S.A.

Books by Rita Rainville

Silhouette Romance

Challenge the Devil #313
McCade's Woman #346
*Lady Moonlight #370
Written on the Wind #400
*The Perfect Touch #418
The Glorious Quest #448
Family Affair #478
It Takes a Thief #502
Gentle Persuasion #535
Never Love a Cowboy #556
Valley of Rainbows #598
*No Way To Treat a Lady #663
Never on Sundae #706
One Moment of Magic #746
*Arc of the Arrow #832
Alone at Last #873
*Too Hard To Handle #1445

Silhouette Desire

A Touch of Class #495
Paid in Full #639
High Spirits #792
Tumbleweed and Gibraltar #828
Hot Property #874
Bedazzled #918
Husband Material #984
City Girls Need Not Apply #1056

Silhouette Books

Silhouette Christmas Stories 1990
"Lights Out!"

*Aunt Tillie stories

RITA RAINVILLE

believes her storytelling ability was honed by her father, a man who told absurd tales with a straight face and a gleam of amusement in his blue eyes. She learned from both parents that laughter, as well as love, makes the world go 'round. Her early years were spent reading every book available and replotting the endings of sad movies.

Rita has been a romantic for as long as she can remember. She began writing romance novels, and continues to this day, because she believes in humor, happy endings and the enduring qualities of love, honor and commitment. She is also spurred on by letters she receives from readers, letters that say things like, "...when I read your books, I laugh out loud and the pain goes away."

Rita is a happily married mother of two super sons, one incredible daughter-in-law and a wonderful grandson. She lives with her husband in northern Arizona.

IT'S OUR 20th ANNIVERSARY!
We'll be celebrating all year,
Continuing with these fabulous titles,
On sale in May 2000.

Chapter One

"Lady, you've got two minutes to get these loonies off my land."

Christy Calhoun's eyes widened as the gaze of the large, tanned man on horseback settled on her. He had scanned her nine companions and the cluster of recreational vehicles scattered around his property before turning to her and issuing the direct order. When he tilted his brown Stetson back off his forehead, she saw that the expression in his narrowed dark eyes was no friendlier than his words.

One quick glance at the older people milling around her resolved her unspoken question. They, in their eye-popping yellow T-shirts each picturing a human waving at a big-eyed alien and the words I'm not Suffering from Alienation, were the loonies; she, in jeans and a white sleeveless T-shirt, was, by default, the lady.

He was more than large, she decided with a blink.

Caught between her and the glare of the late-May sun, he looked very big. Huge. And hard as granite, if the thighs gripping his saddle were any indication. He was, with his broad chest and shoulders wide enough to fill a doorway, more than a tad intimidating.

Before Christy could utter a word, a motor home, the last of their caravan, trundled off the road and up the grassy slope in their direction, smoke pouring out the front grille. Slamming to a stop well behind the other vehicles, the driver leaped out and dashed toward the cluster of people. Before he had gone ten feet, the motor home's chrome grille erupted and flames shot out, blistering the paint and shooting up a plume of dark smoke.

Swearing, the large cowboy swung off his horse and pointed to the hill behind him. "Move," he shouted to the stunned observers. "*Now*. To the other side. The damn thing's going to blow."

Christy took a last look at the blazing motor home then turned to check the people swarming up the hillside. Noting they were all accounted for, she slid her arm protectively around the petite woman beside her. "Come on, Aunt Tillie. The man said to move."

"We'll be fine, dear," the older woman murmured, hiking up her long skirt and obediently trotting up the hill after her friends. "Just fine."

"Not if we don't hustle."

"Oh!" Tillie skidded to a stop and turned back. "My bracelet. It's gone."

Halting beside her, Christy wrapped her fingers around her aunt's wrist and tugged. "Come on, it'll be there when we get back."

"But it's Walter's. I mean, the one he gave me. His last gift."

Christy closed her eyes and sighed. After four days on the road with her lovable, exasperating aunt, she recognized the determination beneath her breathy voice. Come hell or high water, Tillie would go back for that bracelet. "Where is it?"

"There." Tillie pointed to a spot twenty feet behind them where the gold band glittered in the sun.

"I'll get it. You keep moving." Christy nudged her aunt toward the others and waited until they crested the hill before she turned back.

From behind them, Shane McBride watched with mingled fury and disbelief as the trim redhead reversed herself and dashed back toward him and the inferno. Not on my land, he thought grimly, angling to cut her off. No way. She might be a UFO-hunting trespasser, but if she was hurt on his property, she could tie him up in a legal snarl for months. He launched himself at her just as the RV exploded.

A gust of hot air hit him with the force of a sledgehammer, throwing him off balance just as he snagged her. Fiery cinders rained on his back.

Shifting his weight to break the redhead's fall, Shane rolled with her across the grass, coming to a stop with her pinned beneath him. He held her there, hip to hip, sinking into her softness, waiting for the adrenaline to stop roaring through his body, feeling the swell of her breasts press against his chest.

Instead of rolling aside and tugging her to her feet, pure physical appreciation kept him where he was a few seconds longer than necessary. It had obviously been too long since he'd been with a woman, he thought wryly, because she felt damn good. Way too good.

Struggling for air, she shoved at his shoulders. "I can't...breathe." Looking up, she blinked at the lick of flame in the man's dark eyes, so close to her own. It was gone in an instant. Muttering a curse, he shifted to her side, rising to his feet with a fluid power that had her blinking again. It took her longer to move. His hard body had imprinted itself on hers, and she shivered at the aftereffect of heat, flexing muscles and a bar of rigid flesh pressing into her belly.

He leaned over her, extending a large hand. Waiting until her fingers touched his palm, he tightened his grip and pulled her smoothly to her feet. "Are you hurt?"

"No." Dazed by her racing pulse and the heat from his body, but not hurt. Christy shook her head as she looked around the grassy knoll. "I'm fine. I think." Taking in the bits of twisted metal and smoldering grass, she shivered and turned back to him, impulsively squeezing the hand she still held. "Thanks for your help. I'm Christy Calhoun, and I'm really sorry about all this." She gestured vaguely at the shambles around them. "I know it sounds crazy, but I was after my aunt's bracelet, not trying to get blown up."

Turning away to conceal his aroused state, he scowled at the gaggle of older people at the top of the hill then down at her. "Shane McBride. I own this land. If you haven't figured it out yet, you're trespassing."

"Welcome to my world," Christy muttered.

"No, ma'am, you've got that wrong." His deep voice had an edge of lethal softness. "There's no welcome on this ranch for trespassers or idiots looking for UFOs. I've had all the broken fences, burned grass and campers that I intend to deal with. So I'd advise you to turn your cute little butt around, go back out the same cut fence you came in and travel on down the road."

Looking around at the disaster area, she said, "*We* didn't cut the fence. It was already down."

"I know," he said with strained patience. "It was done yesterday by a tourist who claimed he was running away from a UFO. He zigzagged on and off the road and took down nearly a quarter mile of fence. *My* fence."

"Well, we won't do anything like that," she assured him, lifting her hands in a universal gesture of innocence. "Honest, we're really a law-abiding group of..." He half turned, raising his brows when she stopped, flushing, apparently remembering where she was.

"What I mean is, we didn't *know* we were trespassing when we pulled over. We thought it was open land since...there wasn't a fence." As her words dwindled away beneath his skeptical gaze, Christy's thoughts darted to her aunt who, as leader and navigator of the group, had made the decision to stop precisely where they were.

Aunt Tillie.

A nasty suspicion drew her thoughts even further back to a conversation she'd had with one of her cousins two weeks earlier.

Brandy would know what to do, she had thought

at the time, waiting for her cousin to answer the phone. After all, hadn't Brandy been the latest victim among the cousins? Hadn't she—

At the sound of a sunny contralto greeting, Christy had said, "Brandy? Thank God!"

"Christy? Hey, I've been meaning to call. How's the fiancé?"

"Ex-fiancé. But that's not why—"

"Ex?" Brandy cleared her throat. "Isn't that the third man you…? Never mind. How's the job going?"

"Gone, but that's not why—"

"Gone? When?"

"Actually, the same day I got rid of fiancé number three. I was more upset about the job."

"But you've been writing for that magazine for the last two years."

"Yep, but it got caught up in a merger, and it's dead meat," Christy said succinctly. "Brandy, that's not why—"

"So what are you going to do?"

This time, Christy's sigh was long and loud. She should have known she wouldn't control this conversation; she never did when talking with her cousin. "Sorry," she said quickly. "I'm a little stressed here. When my magazine bit the dust, the editor of a travel magazine called me with an offer."

"Christy, that's terrific!"

"You haven't heard about my first assignment."

"Nothing can be that bad," her cousin said in a firm voice. "In the major scheme of things, a year isn't that long."

"A *day* can be that long if I'm working with Aunt Tillie."

"Working with...?"

"Aunt Tillie," Christy confirmed grimly. A fey, spry, enchanting, adventurous, hair-raising dynamo of a woman. A woman fascinated by aliens and UFOs and...a psychic. She had daily conversations with Uncle Walter, a man whose exuberant spirit was apparently undaunted by the insignificant fact that he had passed on to another plane years earlier. She was also a matchmaker, who wreaked havoc in the life of any niece or nephew unfortunate enough to become the object of her attention.

But that had all been family lore, at least as far as Christy was concerned. Born into a military family that moved with regularity, she'd had only intermittent contact with her infamous aunt. So minimal, in fact, that she had always thought the stories were highly exaggerated.

Until this past year.

"She's gathered a herd of senior citizen extraterrestrial believers and organized them into a caravan. The plan is to visit the Nevada and Arizona hot spots of UFO sightings. The seniors, of course, fully expect to find proof of visitations."

"Good grief."

"My thought exactly. And since my first assignment is to write an article on seniors traveling together, I got stuck with Aunt Tillie and her goofy friends."

After a thoughtful pause, her cousin asked cautiously, "How'd your editor know about Aunt Tillie?"

"She didn't. But Mom certainly does. Among other things, she said I couldn't turn Aunt Tillie loose on the rest of the world in an RV."

"Aunt Tillie got her *driver's license* back?" Horror lifted Brandy's voice a notch.

"Last week."

"Good grief."

"Yeah, that's what I thought. So, with the family breathing down my neck and designating me as the sacrificial lamb, I cleared the idea with my editor. She thought it might have a nice, light touch. I'm leaving in about ten days."

Before her cousin could recover, Christy circled back to the original reason for the call. "Brandy, have you ever heard Aunt Tillie call me her little wanderer?"

"Sure. Not lately, but all the time when we were kids. I figured it was because you always meandered away and the family had to send search parties out for you."

"Yeah, I did too."

"Did? Past tense? Not now?"

"No indeedy. She said something yesterday that put a whole new light on the subject."

"Don't tell me. Aliens again?"

"What's *with* her, Brandy? The woman is obsessed with E.T.s. Now she seems to think I'm one of them."

"Oh boy. Did you ask Aunt Tillie about it?"

"You bet your sweet patootie I did."

"And?"

"She said she knew the moment I was born that I was what UFO buffs call a wanderer. She's just been waiting for me to bloom. Damn it, Brandy, this isn't funny. I don't *want* to bloom."

Her cousin's snort of laughter was not comforting. "You're doomed, Christy. There's not a darned thing any of us can do when she goes into high gear. One consolation, though, she'll find you a husband—one who's good with aliens, of course. That's always a top priority with her. After all, she's still convinced she married me off to a real, honest-to-God E.T. Just be grateful that Uncle Walter isn't involved."

"I don't *want* a husband, especially one who hangs around with aliens. I've sworn off men. Three ex-fiancés are more than enough for any woman. And the thought of Uncle Walter sending me messages from the great beyond is the stuff of nightmares," Christy said with a shudder. "Good grief, the man has been dead for at least fourteen years. Is he *ever* going to quit talking to her?"

"Has she mentioned his opinion of your wandering soul or a husband?"

"Well..."

Her cousin's laughter was no longer muffled. "Doomed, Christy. That's what you are. Doomed!"

Earlier, other cousins had laughingly warned her that she, too, would one day be drawn into her aunt's sphere of influence. And her life would never be the same.

Just as they'd predicted, it had happened. The fateful meeting had taken place one rainy afternoon a year earlier, after her move to San Diego, not far from her aunt's home in Rancho Santa Fe. Less than an hour into the visit Christy had been hooked. Enchanted by the tiny woman who loved so openly, she became her staunch supporter and as fiercely protective of her as the rest of the family.

Now, wincing as she remembered Brandy's prediction, Christy tried to rein in her overactive imagination. Granted, this stop had not been on their itinerary; they had been scheduled to drive another fifty miles similar to the last hundred since leaving Las Vegas. Miles of heat-shimmering road carved through stark landscape covered with chaparral and dotted with stumpy Joshua trees and yucca.

True, Aunt Tillie had been sitting beside her in the passenger seat humming a bit off-key when she'd spotted the lush oasis ahead—which coincided with the end of the barbed wire fence—and directed her to pull off the road onto the grassy slope.

But there was no way that Aunt Tillie could have known a man like Shane McBride would be here.

Absolutely none.

This stop was definitely just a spur-of-the-moment thing, she reassured herself. It had nothing to do with Shane, nothing to do with aliens. And definitely nothing to do with husbands.

Nada.

Relieved, she gazed up at Shane and shivered as she felt an involuntary tug of attraction. He did bear a startling resemblance to her three ex-fiancés. Not in physical looks, although they had all been large, solid men, but in his aura of power and control. Of course, it was that very aura that had been the problem.

Three times.

Number one owned a computer company, number two a marketing firm, number three was a real estate broker. All three men were aggressive types whose companies were leaving their competitors in the dust. Unfortunately, they handled their personal lives with the same drive, and she had always been a sucker for the self-assertive types.

But, that was then and this was now—and there was a limit. She had sworn off powerful men. For good. Especially the strong, silent types who assumed control as if by divine right; they were nothing but trouble. She had once believed she could tap into their gentler side, touch the tenderness she thought was just beneath the surface, but three bad experiences had finally opened her eyes.

Men like that were drawn to her generous spirit and open affection, just as she had been drawn to their strength, but it was the old water-and-oil combination. It had taken a while, but she had finally learned her lesson. If she ever started looking for a man again, and that was a big *if,* it would definitely be for a sensitive, caring type.

So if, through some convoluted mental process, Aunt Tillie had concluded that Shane McBride was connected to aliens or would make a terrific nephew-in-law, she could just think again. In fact, the best plan would be to get Tillie back on the road so the matter could die a natural death.

Her eyes narrowed in thought, Christy glanced again at Shane just as he turned to check on the older people walking down the hill.

"Look," she said in a determined voice, "I'll do my best to get this crew on the road. In the meantime, if it makes you feel any better, you can be as rude to me as you like, but when you talk to my aunt, I hope you have the courtesy to—'' She caught her breath, almost choking. ''Good grief, your *shirt*.''

He looked over his shoulder at her. ''What about it?''

''It's burned. And so is your back.'' Shock lifted her voice a notch. ''Why on earth didn't you say something?''

He shrugged. ''I had other things on my mind.''

Yeah, like rescuing her, she thought with a stab of guilt. Giving his sleeve a tug, she said, ''Come on, I have some ointment in the motor home. It'll keep you from blistering.''

In less than two minutes, Shane was sitting on a stool hastily pulled outside with his shirt on his lap to cover his reaction to his nurse, while Christy dabbed a cooling salve on his burns. The touch of her soft hands on his back didn't help a bit. Seconds later, the seniors milled around him, offering sympathy and suggestions. His foreman, Hank Withers, a quiet man, tall and spare, joined them, dismounting behind the group, quieting his mare and Shane's gelding.

Tillie, wearing raspberry tennies, pulled up a camp chair and plunked it in front of Shane. When she sat, her long purple gathered skirt, held up by green suspenders, pooled around her feet. Leaning over, she plucked his shirt from his hands, shook out the dust and spread it across her lap, looking with interest at the logo on the pocket. She drew a slim finger across a swirl of stars with the word Galaxy embroidered in red beneath it.

Flexing the shoulder on which Christy was doctoring a raw spot, he said to the older woman, "I'm Shane McBride."

"Of course you are," she assured him earnestly. "Our host." Smiling at Shane, she added, "You can call me Tillie."

Host?

Christy cleared her throat. "Aunt Tillie, Mr. McBride wants us to leave."

Tillie tilted her head, studying Shane before switching her gaze to her niece. "You must have misunderstood, dear. It's the scene of an accident. Nobody leaves. At least, not until the insurance people come." Her brows drew together in thought. "Or perhaps it's the rental people—or the police. And, who knows, that could be several days."

Beaming at Shane, she said, "When you lowered the fence for us, I knew we were meant to pull over for a rest."

Christy stiffened. "Aunt Tillie, the fence was broken by a man who claims he was being chased by a UFO."

"Wonderful! I *knew* we were in the right place." Her eyes sparkled with delight.

Shane wanted to scowl to show he meant business, but there was something about her expectant look, her bright blue eyes and mop of silver curls that stopped him. It would have been like taking a potshot at Tinkerbell. "No, ma'am, I don't think wonderful's quite the word. He was as drunk as a skunk."

She twinkled at him, clasping his shirt to her chest. "Just think! Actually chased by a UFO. We expect to have the same good luck. Don't we?'' she asked, turning to her friends for confirmation.

They nodded, apparently sharing her enthusiasm. The only exception to the general fervor, Shane noted, was the very curvy lady with the mass of red hair who was still dabbing at his back. She just sighed.

"Lovely shirt.'' Tillie handed it back to Shane and waved at the group assembled around her. "These are my friends. They release water, read palms, hunt and catch people, fly, gamble, fix things, open minds and create.''

Still grappling with the idea of being host to a gathering of UFO hunters, especially those with the qualifications just revealed by their fluttering leader, Shane got to his feet and shrugged on his shirt.

Christy dropped the ointment back into the box of medical supplies and slid between Shane and the seniors. They were a formidable group, individually or collectively, she realized, and it made no sense at all, but she still felt as protective about them as she did Tillie. No doubt it had to do with what the family called her nurturing nature—or an addled mental state resulting from too much contact with her aunt.

"Shane,'' she said hastily, "I'd like you to meet our resident dowser.''

A diminutive woman with graying brown hair stepped forward and gave his hand a firm shake. "Ruth Ann Watts. Glad to meet you.''

Christy gestured to a tall, slim man with eyes like blue lasers. "The man who catches people.''

Remaining where he was, leaning against a tree trunk, the man nodded. "Jack Beatty, retired cop.''

Another gesture from Christy. "The man who *hunts* for people."

"Search and rescue," a small, wiry man in dark glasses explained. "Claude Rollins."

Waving a couple forward who resembled Jack Sprat and his wife, Christy said, "Skip and Opal Williams."

Skip gave an amiable nod. Opal bustled forward, pumping Shane's hand. "My husband's a mechanic, and I read palms." Before she stepped back beside Skip, she turned Shane's hand over and took a quick peek at it.

A portly, bald man reached out to shake Shane's hand. "Jim Sturgiss, retired Air Force. Howdy."

"Ben Matthews." Short and muscular as a wrestler, the next man nodded. "I'm the creative one," he said, dry humor lacing his deep voice.

Grinning at the baffled expression in Shane's eyes, Christy touched a tall woman in jeans and cowboy boots on the shoulder. "Our gambler."

"Melinda Rills," the tall woman said, echoing Christy's amused smile. "Stock market and casinos."

The last man stepped forward and extended his hand. Pale and pudgy, he was obviously still reeling from the explosion. "Dave Davidson, the one who opens minds. I'm a retired psychology teacher, and I don't usually go around blowing things up. I'm sorry this happened on your property."

"Well, Boss, if I was a bettin' man, I could've lost ten bucks back there. I never thought you'd let them stay."

"It's only for a couple of days," Shane muttered, as he and Hank headed toward the barn. "At the most."

He wasn't sure what had happened. Maybe the explosion had rattled his brain. Or it was Tillie looking at him as if he were her last hope for salvation. Or Christy. Hell, he didn't know. With all of them talking at once, assuring him that they would clean up the area while they waited for the rental people, it had been hard to think.

Partly, though, it was Tillie. The little woman with the weird clothes and incandescent smile had worked some sort of magic. The others he could have kicked off the property without a qualm, but not Tillie.

And, as much as he disliked the idea, not Christy. Not the redhead. Just one look at her had his body on red alert, and that was asking for trouble. Big trouble. Even worse had been the feeling of instant recognition that had poured through every cell of his body when he'd first seen her. If he'd believed in fate or destiny, he would have conceded that she was the one woman he'd been looking for all of his life.

But he wasn't a dreamer. Two women who had liked his money a hell of a lot more than they'd liked him had helped him grow up fast. And he didn't believe in fate—at least not where a wife was concerned. None of the women he'd met had ever been right. Not for a lifetime. He doubted one existed. But, damn, at first glance she sure came close.

"How much of the fence did you fix?" he asked abruptly, deliberately changing the direction of his thoughts.

"Not much." Hank shrugged his lean shoulders.

"After the explosion, Milt, here," he nodded at the gelding, "came flying over the hill and it took me a while to catch him."

"We'll head back tomorrow and finish up."

"What about them?" Hank gestured over his shoulder at the people milling around the motor homes, his hazel eyes questioning.

"We'll leave that one section of fence open for them."

"What about the herd?"

"We'll have to wait to move it in there until they're gone." Shane dismounted when they reached the barn. "Who's cooking tonight?"

"Red." Hank sighed. "Beans again. You know, we're gonna have a mutiny on our hands if we don't get another cook out here. And don't even suggest Adelaide. Half of us got food poisoning the one time she tried."

"Yeah. I know." Remembering, Shane winced. The housekeeper was a jewel, but not in the kitchen. "I've called all the temp agencies in Vegas, but the odds of finding someone are slim to none. Anyone who can cook for more than one person at a time has been snatched up for the summer by dude ranches or local camps. And Hector called this morning with more bad news after he pulled into Dallas. Said his dad is worse off than he thought, and he'd probably have to stay two or three weeks."

Hank groaned. "A couple of days without a cook is bad enough, but two or three *weeks*? Boss, you gotta do something." Taking the reins from Shane's hand, he said, "I'll take care of the horses, you go make a miracle."

An hour later, Shane closed the telephone directory with an irritated thump. Nothing. There wasn't a cook to be found in the whole damn county.

Maybe there was hope for Shane after all.

Christy braked to a stop and hopped off her bicycle at the front gate, looking at the gracious old house surrounded by lush, well-tended grass. It was no Tara, but then she had always thought such magnificence was overrated. This was a home—pale creamy yellow, two stories, with a wraparound porch that was cozily furnished with an oak swing and wicker chairs punctuated with bright floral cushions. Enclosed by a white rail with gently curved spindles, it all but shouted a welcome. It was the kind of home she had dreamed about as a child moving from place to place. It was a deeply feminine house, she reflected, for such a hard man.

But a man who appreciated a home like this couldn't be all bad, she thought. Not that she was interested on a personal level, of course, but she made a point of giving credit where it was due. And he did appreciate it; it showed in the recent paint job, the tidy shrubbery, the profusion of pink and white flowers tumbling here and there.

Shane walked around the corner and caught her gazing dreamy-eyed at the house. With her hand on the gate of the picket fence, she had the tranquil look of a woman coming home. She looked nice there. She looked…right.

Taking a deep breath, he shook his head. No way was he going down *that* road. With her green eyes, high cheekbones and full mouth, Christy was one hell of a looker. Her blazing mass of red-gold hair didn't hurt, either. But she was going to be here two days, tops, and he could manage to keep his hands off her for that long. Maybe. Pushing down the surge of lust that slammed through him, he strode toward her. It would be helpful if his imagination would just simmer down, he thought, muttering a quiet oath. Mighty helpful.

Pulling the gate open, he scowled at her flushed face. "It's almost a hundred degrees out here and dry as dirt. What the hell are you doing on a bike? Without a hat?" When her narrowed eyes glittered with irritation, he heaved a sigh. "Can I get you something cold to drink, iced tea, beer?"

Christy ran her hands through her hair to control both it and her temper. "First, a bike is convenient," she snapped. "Second, I don't need a caretaker, and third, no thank you. My aunt wants to be sure you know how much we all appreciate being able to stay here, and—"

"All?"

Taking a deep breath and releasing it, she nodded. "All." She gave an exasperated sigh. "All right, I'm not thrilled about it, but you *were* kind—"

"Kind?" His brows rose.

"And courteous to my aunt and her friends," she said through clenched teeth, "and I am grateful for that. Can I get on with this?" she asked, stopping him before he could interrupt again.

"So they asked me to tell…I mean we want to invite you to dinner to show our appreciation."

A corner of his mouth kicked up in a slow smile. "This is killing you, isn't it?"

"You bet." Tightening her grip on the handlebars, Christy backed up a cautious step. His grin was a lethal weapon, she decided, and it shouldn't be aimed at unsuspecting women. Reminding herself that she was immune to his brand of charm, she asked abruptly, "Are you coming or not?"

"I wouldn't miss it for the world."

Chapter Two

"More than likely, the RV had a ruptured fuel line," Skip said. "It happens every now and then. Smoke, flames, a big boom and bingo—you got nothing left."

"Dowsing is simple," Ruth Ann commented to Jack with a grin. "Even a cynical cop can do it. You don't need anything fancy, a forked stick does the trick. Willow works well."

"Keno loves her job." Claude ran a hand over the German shepherd's head, pausing to scratch behind the erect ears. "And she's damn good at it, too."

Shane sat in the same camp chair he'd been in earlier, only this time he held a bottle of beer and listened to the fragments of conversation coming from the clusters of people around him.

His guests.

Some were setting the two long tables in the center of the clearing for dinner. They had a rhythm, as if they'd been doing it for weeks rather than just four days. Others lounged in chairs, idly chatting.

They had cleaned the area as promised, he had noted as he'd ridden Milt into the hollow. The debris had been tossed in a heap near the carcass of the burned RV, and the rest of the motor homes encircled the large area obviously pinpointed for community activities.

As before, Tillie sat across from him, her yellow alien shirt complemented by the green suspenders. His lips twitched as she beamed at him, her approval as obvious as the setting sun. She seemed especially taken with his shirt, a duplicate of the denim one he'd worn earlier. Of course, she seemed fascinated by a number of things; she just didn't make much sense when she talked about them.

Amused, he decided to see if he'd have better luck with another subject. Any subject. "What are you thinking about?"

"Cows."

Shane blinked. "Cows?" Could've fooled him. He was sure she had shirts on her mind.

"*Your* cows." She gave him a quick look.

"Cattle," he said absently, wondering at the sudden shift of emotions playing across her face. Anxiety had replaced approval.

"The ones here," she clarified.

"By 'here,' do you mean on the ranch?"

"No, right here." Tillie pointed a slim finger at the ground, then waved vaguely, encompassing the area around them. "Walter mentioned…that is, he thought…the cows might not be happy. Of course, you don't have…at least, not yet."

Determined not to laugh, Shane settled for clearing his throat and selecting a word from the maze. "Uh…happy?"

"Here," she repeated.

He gave up. Grinning at her earnest expression, he looked around, wondering if there was an interpreter in the group. *Happy? Cows?* "Well," he said slowly, "it's not real easy to tell how they feel. Actually, I think they're fine as long as they have good grass and water. That's why I'll be moving them down here. It's also one of the reasons I was fixing the fence."

"They wouldn't…like it over there?" She pointed over the hills behind them.

Shane shrugged. "Who knows? But they won't crowd you," he promised, hoping to erase the crease between her brows. "I'll wait until you're gone before I move them in." He blinked, narrowing his eyes at her. "Who's Walter?"

"Perhaps it would be better if…" Her words faded away, then she brightened and leaned forward to pat his hand. "But I wouldn't worry. Walter says— Oh good, it won't be long now."

Shane's brows rose at the cryptic statement. Worry? About what? And what wouldn't be long? Until they were gone? His stomach rumbled, reminding him that breakfast had been early and lunch nonexistent.

"Until we eat," Tillie said matter-of-factly.

Just then, the door of the nearest motor home opened, releasing an aroma that made his mouth water. One thing was certain, he decided: beans weren't on the menu.

"Dinner's ready," Christy called.

Ruth Ann, Jack and Claude trooped over to the door and returned with large, covered dishes. After depositing them on the tables, they went back for more.

Tillie grabbed Shane's sleeve. "Come on. Walter always says the end of the table is best. Less confusion."

Shrugging, Shane rose and allowed himself to be tugged along. Tillie sat at his right, nodding when Christy slid in on his left side. Within seconds he was surrounded by UFO hunters silently passing plates of food. His guests, he reminded himself again.

He took a bite of tender Swiss steak, closed his eyes and savored it while his taste buds broke into the *Hallelujah Chorus*.

Christy's brows rose at his awed expression. "Did you think we invited you for burned hamburgers?"

"The way I've been eating lately, I would've enjoyed even that. But this, it's..."

"Wonderful? Extraordinary? Phenomenal?"

He nodded. "All of the above."

"I'd like to take the credit, but this is my week to be scullery maid. Ben's the magician." She pointed to the short, muscular man with a gray crew cut. "He only lets me wash and cut veggies."

"He cooks for everyone?"

She nodded. "Dinner only. We're on our own for breakfast and lunch."

"How'd you con him into that?"

Christy turned to look at Ben, her expression thoughtful. "I'm not sure. It was a done deal before

I came along, but I think he was bored silly. He'd recently retired as head chef from a really great restaurant and cooking just for himself wasn't cutting it. As it is, he can produce a meal like this easier than I can make a batch of cookies.''

''You don't say.'' Shane gazed at the muscular wizard, knowing his luck had just changed. A real live chef, a *bored* chef, was sitting across the table from him, and he was damn well going to do whatever it took to keep him right here. For at least three weeks.

Of course, if he kept the cook, he'd more than likely have to keep the rest of them. They seemed to be a package deal. Glancing around the table at the yellow-shirted bunch, he sighed. The thought of them running tame on his land searching for UFOs was enough to turn his hair gray, but hell, he could control them. What was important was talking Ben Matthews into cooking until Hector returned. Wondering if immediately after dinner was too soon to tell Ben that the Circle M would gladly help ease the strain of his retirement, Shane reached again for the platter of Swiss steak.

He stopped chewing when another thought occurred to him. If they stayed, Christy stayed. And that changed everything. If she wasn't leaving in two days, he could do something about the fire that flooded his body every time he looked at her. Hell, who was he kidding? Every time he *thought* of her. Turning to look down at her wispy bangs and glorious mass of hair, he held back a smile. Yeah, his luck had definitely changed.

When her elbow brushed Shane's arm again,

Christy shifted her chair a bit to the left. It was one thing to make nice with the man, entirely another to sit so close she was scorched by the heat radiating from his big body.

She would do a lot for Aunt Tillie, but being agreeable to him wasn't easy. He was too much like her three exes—high-handed and forceful. Of course a lot of men faced with an exploding RV and a gaggle of UFO hunters on their property would probably react the same way.

Even so, he was dangerous. Of course, it wasn't his fault that she was wary of men—especially the alpha types. Or that what she craved right now was a peaceful life, a life dedicated to her new job and simple pleasures. A life rid of complications—especially the ones created by demanding men.

She hadn't been a bit interested when he'd taken off his shirt so she could deal with his back, she assured herself. Yeah, right. The sight of his hard body hadn't doubled her pulse rate either, and his heat hadn't sizzled through her fingertips, warming her from head to toe.

She was accustomed to attractive men. All three of her exes had been disciplined, keeping their bodies in first-rate condition. Health, number two had told her, was a big advantage in beating down the competition. And they had muscles. Plenty of them. So there had been no reason for her to gape at Shane like a hormone-crazed teenager. She should be able to take broad shoulders, a wide chest lightly sprinkled with dark hair, and a flat, hard stomach in stride.

So he was spectacular. So what? He was still a royal pain. He was the prototype of all the troublesome men who had caused her to swear *off* men, for heaven's sake.

Grateful they would be leaving in a day or so, she decided she could be polite until then. It couldn't be that difficult, despite the waves of tension radiating from him. Noting that Tillie was complimenting Ben on the dinner, she turned to Shane.

"How's your—"

"Who is—"

They both stopped, waiting.

"You first," Shane said, leaning back when Melinda reached over his shoulder to collect his plate.

"I just wanted to know if your back is bothering you. I have plenty of ointment if you—"

He shook his head. "No thanks. It stings a little, but it'll be fine by tomorrow."

"Okay." Her voice was cool. "Now it's your turn."

Nodding toward the cluster of seniors, Shane asked, "Which one is Walter?"

A chill shot straight up Christy's spine. "Walter?" Her voice cracked midword.

Peering around him at her aunt, who was comparing notes with Opal, the palmist, Christy groped for a response. Tillie had no inhibition about quoting Walter—anytime, anywhere, with anyone. It was perfectly reasonable for Shane to want him identified.

It was also a problem because there was no reasonable explanation for Walter—especially to a man who already thought they were a bunch of lunatics.

"Walter is...Aunt Tillie's husband," she said, opting for truthful evasion for as long as she could.

Even the verb was honest because, unfortunately, there was nothing past tense about the blasted man. Except his body.

"I don't remember meeting him."

She shook her head, deliberately ignoring his puzzled expression. "You didn't. He...couldn't come on this trip."

"Then why was he talking about my cattle?"

Choking on a sip of iced tea, Christy asked weakly, "Your cattle? You sure it was Walter?"

"That's what Tillie said."

"Exactly *what* did she say?"

"Something about my cattle not being happy in this hollow."

"Oh." A nasty vision of cows keeling over by the dozens ran through her mind, then she looked around and brightened. "You don't *have* any cows here."

"Not yet. But they'll be here as soon as you leave."

She angled a quick glance at him before concentrating on her perspiring glass of tea. "Uh...you couldn't wait a while before moving them?"

"Why? I want to do it before they overgraze the area they're in."

"No particular reason." Except that there was usually some sort of logic—absurd or otherwise— behind Uncle Walter's suggestions.

"I don't get it." Shane turned to face her, his wide shoulders concealing the people behind him. "If he isn't here, how could he know about my ranch? And why would he care?"

Give the man a cigar. He had some good questions. "Aunt Tillie probably described the place to him," she said vaguely, checking her options again. So much for honesty. It never lasted long when the subject was Tillie or her talkative mate. Two days, she reminded herself. Just a measly forty-eight hours and they'd be on their way. And being around Tillie had taught her a few things; she could dodge his curiosity and pointed questions for that long.

Shane gave her a last, exasperated look before turning to the man across the table. "Ben, that was a wonderful meal. I wonder if we could talk for a minute."

Tillie turned to face him, her eyes gleaming with satisfaction.

Not trusting her aunt's look of anticipation, Christy felt the chill skitter back down her spine.

Ben leaned back in his chair, arms crossed on his chest, and nodded.

"I need a good cook for about three weeks," Shane said bluntly. "What can I do to interest you in the job?" Listening in dismay while he explained, Christy looked from one face to the next with a sinking feeling. No one jumped up to violently object. No one even looked upset.

"How many men do you have?" Ben asked.

"Ten."

"What's your kitchen like?"

"It was remodeled last year with commercial appliances."

Ben shrugged. "I'm listening."

Christy groaned at the avid interest in Ben's brown eyes as he heard the details. The blasted man couldn't wait to get back in a hot kitchen with twenty pans going at once.

"I could do it." Ben's words were measured as carefully as the ingredients in his sauces. "But we're all together on this trip. If I stay, we all stay; it has to be a group decision. And I still cook dinner for everyone here."

Shane gave a brief nod. "I figured that. Do you want me to leave so you can talk it over?"

"No need. We're not shy." Turning to the others, Ben said, "What do you think?"

Doomed. Christy slumped in her chair, remembering her cousin's words as they all gazed at Tillie. But it was only fair they defer to her, she reminded herself. After all, the trip *had* been Tillie's idea. She had determined the itinerary, announced it on the Internet and found compatible people. Each of them doted on her, recognized her special ability and would follow her through the gates of hell. It didn't take a psychic to know what her aunt's decision would be, Christy thought gloomily.

"How wonderful!" Tillie beamed a smile at each of them. "We're exactly where we are meant to be." Sliding a glance at Shane, she added, "Practically at the door of Area 51."

Christy's groan was lost in the excited conversation. She wondered how she had lived her entire life—before Aunt Tillie—without hearing of the famed Area 51 and the Nellis Air Force Base Bombing and Gunnery Range. While the Air Force had recently, and reluctantly, acknowledged that it had "operations" at Area 51, it still wouldn't reveal what was happening there.

Skeptics believed that the government was testing exciting new jets that looked bizarre because they were experimental. UFO buffs believed the government had captured alien spacecraft and had made, and were testing, their own spaceships. There was no doubt which angle *these* people subscribed to.

The general area had been designated on their itinerary as the first major "hot spot" to be investigated, with a proposed stay of three weeks.

Jack grinned at Tillie. "Are you suggesting we use the ranch as a base of operations?"

"If it's agreeable with everyone." Tillie took another peek at Shane's face and nodded, satisfied.

"Why not?" Ruth Ann looked at each of them, inviting comments. When there were none, she turned to Ben. "Of course, how much loot you can squeeze out of Shane is strictly your own business."

Ben got up, looking across the table at his new boss. "Looks like you might have a deal."

"Good. Before we take a walk and settle things, I have one more suggestion." His quick glance, resting on Christy's resigned expression for a moment, included them all. "How about moving closer to the house? I have an empty bunkhouse you can park by. You'll probably want to stay in your RVs, but you can use the tubs and showers in the cabin."

Again, all heads swiveled toward Tillie.

She nodded and touched Ben's arm. "You go right now. The rest of us will stay here for...a while."

Shane frowned. "It'll be nicer for you near the house."

Patting his hand, Tillie said, "Your home is lovely. We'll be there." She looked skyward for a moment, then gave a definite nod. "Day after tomorrow, Wednesday morning before the storm gets too bad.''

"What storm?" Shane turned a puzzled frown on Christy. "We're not expecting rain."

Avoiding his gaze, she muttered, "Don't look at me. I'm the last one around here to know anything."

Five minutes later the two men returned from a short walk, their satisfied expressions clear to the rest of the group.

Shane tucked a cellular phone back in his shirt pocket. "Hank says he'll meet you at the gate in an hour and lead you in."

Ben nodded, moving toward his motor home.

Reaching for Christy's hand, Shane tugged gently, bringing her to her feet. "Let's go."

She scowled and tried to sink back into the chair. "Where?"

"Out there." Shane kept her at his side as he gestured toward the surrounding hills. Any damn where at all, as long as they were far away from the voluble alien hunters still clustered around the tables.

Hesitating, Christy cast a glance at her aunt, who was again chatting with Opal. It wasn't a smart move to wander away with a man who practically had a large *T* branded on his forehead. Trouble was something she didn't need, and caring for a small, elderly aunt was always a good excuse.

"You go on, dear. Enjoy yourself." Tillie waved absently in her direction. "I'm just fine."

Shane slid his arm around her waist and nudged her toward an opening in the circle of RVs before she could use the deepening darkness as another excuse.

Stopping by a tall juniper, he looked down at her. "Did you tell Tillie about my house?"

"Nope. I started scrubbing veggies as soon as I got back."

"Then how does she know what it looks like?"

Christy stopped to look up at him. "Beats me. She just seems to know these things." So much for trying to deceive him with half-truths, she reflected with resignation. For a couple of days, there might have been a chance. But not for three weeks. And she had a gut feeling that Shane would not be a happy man when he learned that he was not only hosting a troupe of UFO hunters but a genuine, dyed-in-the-wool psychic.

He tightened his arm and kept her moving over the grass while he considered her aunt. "It doesn't make sense," he finally said. "And there's no storm coming. I checked the weather channel before I rode over here for dinner."

Loosening the large hand at her waist with a sigh, Christy stepped away from him. "Look, if you're going to be around Aunt Tillie for any length of time, you might as well understand something." It still wasn't easy to explain, she reflected. Even after a year of practice. "She's, uh..."

"She's what?"

"You won't believe it," she hedged. "No one ever does—at least not at first."

Drawing her closer, he casually draped his arm over her shoulder. "I'll believe it," he promised.

"I doubt it." Get it over with, she told herself. Now. "She's...psychic."

His hand tightened on her shoulder and after a

moment she looked up at him. His expression was typical, she reflected. Tolerant and a bit patronizing. The look most men gave her before explaining that only the gullible and weak-minded believed in mediums.

"I don't mean just a little, either," she added for good measure. "She's an absolute, out-and-out, mind-boggling psychic."

"I don't believe it." He scowled down at her.

"Isn't that exactly what I told you?" she muttered in exasperation.

Shane ran a hand through his hair, leaving it rumpled and standing in spikes. This wasn't the conversation he'd planned to have once he got Christy alone. Their two days had been stretched to three weeks, but it wouldn't mean a damn thing if she tossed verbal bombs at him every time they got together.

"Look, I've already got a bunch of E.T. hunters on my hands, you don't have to add a fortune-teller." He took a deep breath and added in a flat voice, "Besides, I don't believe in psychics."

"How nice for you." Maybe it was the fact that Tillie was surrounded by a legion of protectors and didn't need her added support, Christy thought, but for the first time she could enjoy the absurdity of the situation.

"I didn't either until a year ago, when I settled in San Diego and my relatives stuck me with Aunt Tillie for a weekend. During that time I learned that she doesn't need a security system at her place because she always knows who's approaching her house. I learned that she never uses a telephone book—she just picks up the phone and dials the right numbers."

Shane groaned.

"I learned that she always knows when family and friends are either hurt or in trouble."

Sighing, Shane said, "Let me ask again, who exactly is this Walter?"

Her soft laughter filling the air, Christy said, "Her husband."

"And why isn't he here taking care of her?"

"Because he's dead."

His scowl grew darker. *"Dead?"*

"Yep." She grinned. "Of course, Aunt Tillie says he made his transition, but any way you look at it, he's gone. But not forgotten, no sirree. And believe me, he didn't go quietly. It seems like the man never stops talking. Fourteen years ago," she added before he could ask.

"I don't believe it."

"You already said that."

"Do you have any idea how crazy this sounds?"

"Yeah, I do. Which is why I hate to tell anyone about it, but I thought since we're going to be here a while, you should be warned."

"And he talked to her about my cattle?"

"I wouldn't be surprised." Christy sighed. "He talks to her about almost everything. My mother said his financial advice had tripled her portfolio. Aunt Tillie's, not my mother's," she added with scrupulous honesty.

"So why is this dead man fixated on my cattle?"

"I haven't the foggiest idea. But, believe me, my family jumps when he issues a warning."

"It wasn't a warning," he snapped. "It was just...a comment."

"As far as Uncle Walter is concerned, it's the same thing. I'd pay attention if I were you." Christy turned back toward the RVs. "So now you've had two warnings—one from Walter and one from me."

Shane caught her arm and gently swung her toward him. "Wait a minute. This isn't what I wanted to talk about when we came out here."

Panic swept through her when his voice deepened. "Well of course it isn't," she said brightly. "How could you? You didn't know about it." The fear that he would say something she absolutely, positively did not want to hear kept her talking. "Uncle Walter isn't a topic that many would think of. After all, how many dead men—"

He stopped her by lifting her chin and brushing his lips against hers in a slow, tender kiss. Finally, when the tension left her body and she sagged against him, he raised his head. "I want to talk about us." His dark gaze swept her face before he turned and led her farther away from the lights of the motor homes.

Digging her heels in the soft grass, she pulled away and held up a hand to keep him back. Damned if she hadn't been right about the brand on his forehead; the man was nothing but trouble. Oddly enough, she had forgotten that the letter could also stand for testosterone. As in way too much of it. And she had a nasty hunch that he was as stubborn and relentless as all three exes combined.

"Whoa, cowboy," she said breathlessly. "We've

known each other about six hours. Don't you think you're rushing things a bit?''

He gave a slow shake of his head. ''From my point of view, we've already wasted most of the day.''

Blinking, she took a deep breath to release the tension building inside her. Then, since it hadn't helped much, she took another one and quickly stepped past him, hurrying distractedly back to the RVs. His blunt approach was all too familiar. And, unfortunately for her, there was something morbidly fascinating about the direct, Me-Tarzan, you-Jane method. Even worse, in the past, it had worked. But that was then, she reminded herself. This was now. And things were different.

She was different. She had changed.

She had a batch of new priorities—an interesting job, potential career advancement and, best of all, no forceful men in her life.

Granted, there were a few dangling threads from her old life that needed attention. They were minor. A quick conversation with Aunt Tillie would clear up the wanderer issue. Ignoring the worrisome thought that conversations with her aunt were neither quick nor reasonable, Christy pressed on.

Another more pointed talk with Shane would probably be necessary, but she could handle that.

After all, she *had* changed.

Chapter Three

"Come on, Aunt Tillie, give."

Seated at the motor home's simulated oak table, nibbling at a chicken salad, Christy pondered the difficulties of getting a few minutes alone with her aunt. She hadn't been able to corner Tillie the night before after Shane had left, and today it hadn't been easy to wean her away from the tangle of seniors vociferously debating the methods of breaking through the military guards into Area 51. In fact, it had been impossible. So she had found a shady spot and waited until hunger drove them to their motor homes for lunch. Now, with luck, she'd have an uninterrupted hour devoted to questions and answers.

Tillie tilted her head, reminding Christy of a perky, blue-eyed bird. "Shane is a nice man, isn't he? And subtle. Just look at the shirts he wears."

Nice? Subtle? *Shirts?* The look Christy aimed at her was one of sheer disbelief. "Aunt Tillie, I use words for a living, remember? That means I select them with care, and nice is hardly one I'd choose to describe Shane McBride. Relentless, maybe. Obstinate, definitely. But, nice, subtle? No way. I can think of a lot of words, but none of them have anything to do with nice. And what do his shirts—'' She stopped, a crease forming between her brows as she studied her aunt's artless expression.

"Oh, no you don't, we're not going there," she said firmly. "Your little diversion isn't going to work this time. We're not talking about Shane. What we're discussing here is your affection for all beings extraterrestrial and why you think I'm one of them."

If Christy had learned anything in the past year, it was that being tactful with her aunt was a lost cause. Tillie could be perfectly coherent and logical... unless she was disturbed or simply chose not to discuss a certain topic. When that happened, she was as hard to pin down as a campaigning politician. So tact was not an option here; gritty perseverance was the only thing that seemed to work.

"This wanderer thing," Christy prompted. "I want you to explain it, using plain and simple words. What makes you say that—"

"Your aura."

"My what?"

"It was glorious, vibrant." Tillie clasped her hands to her chest, dazzled by the memory. "Indigo, of course."

"Indigo," Christy repeated in a neutral voice. "Of course." It had happened again. They were less than a minute into a conversation, and she was absolutely lost. Tillie's answers were usually confusing, she reminded herself, but given enough time they—occasionally—eventually made sense. So all she had to do was hang in there. If she was lucky, she might even comprehend what Tillie considered a reasonable explanation.

"And you were only five minutes old." Charmed by the memory, Tillie smiled. Then silver brows drew together in thought. "Ten at the most."

"And from that—"

"Oh, yes." Tillie gave a decisive nod. "I knew."

"But, *how?*" No, Christy thought with resignation, it wasn't going to work. No amount of time would help her understand. Aunt Tillie's thought process was as tangled as her conversation. She didn't know the meaning of linear thinking, didn't have a nodding acquaintance with the normal give-and-take in dialogue. She communicated on some mystical plane that resembled the descending spiral of a corkscrew.

"The color," Tillie prompted.

"Oh, yeah, the indigo."

"Precisely. You know what it means, of course."

"I...uh...think you'd better refresh my memory."

"It's the color of a great humanitarian, one with responsibility for others."

"And that makes me a..."

Her aunt nodded, giving her an encouraging smile. "Walter thought so, too."

Christy stared at her, wondering if Tillie had any idea how the mention of her husband's name could strike terror in the hearts of her family members.

"He was there, of course," Tillie commented, burrowing her fork in the salad to capture a cashew.

Popping it in her mouth, she crunched on it and added, "When you were born. He saw it, too."

"It?" Christy rubbed her forehead with the tips of her fingers, wondering how they had strayed from the subject at hand. Wondering what they were talking about *now*.

"Your aura, dear."

"Oh. And *he* knew?"

"Oh, yes. You had the eyes of an old soul, but it was our secret." She smiled at the reminiscence. "We watched your progress as you grew. Even with your father shifting from one army base to another, taking the family with him, we always knew...."

Deciding she didn't want to know how they kept in touch, Christy settled for another question. "Knew what?"

"That you were developing just as you should."

Heaving a frustrated sigh, she tried again. "Aunt Tillie, just exactly what is a wanderer, and what does one do?"

Tillie looked at the counter behind Christy and said, "Would you hand me the cellular phone, dear?"

Nodding, Christy reached for it and passed it across the table. The phone trilled just as Tillie reached for it.

Nodding her thanks, she smiled. "It's for me."

"I really hate it when you do that." She had experienced a lot with her aunt this past year, but Christy still got a jolt when Tillie pulled that particular stunt. Now, watching, she didn't like the look of growing enthusiasm on the older woman's face. The topic under discussion was, of course, Area 51.

"That's a splendid idea, Jack. I'll be there in two minutes." Handing the phone to Christy, Tillie jumped up, fluffed her long, tangerine skirt, and straightened the bright blue T-shirt that portrayed an E.T. swaggering toward the White House and proclaimed Alien with an Attitude. Blinking with excitement, she said, "Jack thinks he knows how to bust into Area 51!"

Christy hopped up and reached the door before Tillie, blocking it with her body. "Whoa, hold on a minute. I've done some research on the place, Aunt Tillie, and the military doesn't mess around with intruders. They have sensors, big mean guys wearing camouflage uniforms and Blackhawk helicopters. They even have a sign that says that the use of deadly force is authorized. Jack, of all people, should know not to mess with a gang like that."

Tillie patted Christy's cheek and ducked under her arm. "So sweet," she murmured. "Always concerned about others. Don't worry, we'll be fine." She trotted a few steps before stopping to look back over her shoulder. "Dave Davidson won't be at the meeting."

With a sigh, Christy closed the door and leaned back against it, her eyes narrowed in thought. Dave Davidson, she pondered. Tillie's comments, trivial as they often seemed, usually had an underlying message, and if she was pointing in the professor's direction the implication might be that he… Grinning, she turned, pulled the door open—and ran into a body honed to solid muscle by years of hard work.

"Umf," she muttered, her mouth pressed against

Shane's hard chest. His arm clamped her against him, holding her with startling ease.

"Whoa," he murmured. "What's the rush?"

"No rush," she gasped, easing back as much as his grasp allowed. None at all. She was simply going to see the man who might tell her why her aunt believed she was from another planet. No biggie. "I just need to speak to Dave."

"I'll go with you," Shane said, slowly releasing her, his dark gaze skimming her flushed face. "I want to talk to Tillie, but that can wait."

Christy shook her head. The last thing she needed was his company while she talked with Dave. Shane had already decided the bunch of them were lunatics; he didn't need proof to bolster his belief.

"No? You don't want me along?" He waited, holding her there without even touching her.

"It's not that," she told him, mentally cursing her transparent expression and the fact that she couldn't tell a convincing lie. "It's just that Tillie joined the others at Jack's place, and they may be leaving soon." She shrugged. "So if it's important, you'd better catch her while you can."

"It's not all that urgent. I just don't see why she insists on staying down here," he said, clearly exasperated with Tillie's stubborn determination. "You'd all be more comfortable at the house."

"You're right." Christy nodded encouraging him. "I don't know why, either. I think you *should* talk with her. Go to Jack's place and pound on the door. They're probably all yelling at each other about the best way to break into Area 51."

Shane studied her face. "Why do I get the feeling you're trying to get rid of me?"

"Me?" Christy gave innocence her best shot. "Why would I do a thing like that? I just happen to agree with you."

Three minutes later, after watching a suspicious Shane walk through Jack's door, Christy was sitting across from Dave with a glass of iced tea in her hand.

Raising his brows, Dave studied her expression. "Something on your mind?"

"Actually, yes."

"And you're here because I'm irresistible?"

"Well, there is that." Christy's answering smile faded to a thoughtful frown. She seemed to be doing a lot of frowning lately, she reflected as she set her glass carefully on a coaster and wondered how to ask for information without sounding as weird as the rest of them. "Actually, I'm hoping you can answer a few questions for me. Aunt Tillie all but suggested that I come."

"Let me take a wild guess." Dave's brown eyes were both amused and sympathetic. "You want to know about Wanderers, spelled with a capital W." Grinning at Christy's dumbfounded expression, he shook his head. "Don't even think it. I'm not psychic. Tillie's been bragging about her E.T. niece since our first meeting."

"Well, hell." Christy shook her head in disgust. "I suppose you've all heard her version of my birth."

"Yep. Old soul eyes and all."

"And do you believe it?"

Dave shrugged. "I don't know. I don't know what I believe about any of this stuff. In case you haven't figured it out, I'm the token skeptic in the group. I've read everything I could get my hands on—that's what retired teachers do, you know—so I understand what they're all talking about. I just don't know what I believe."

Heaving a sigh of relief, Christy brightened. "That's more objectivity than I expected from anyone in this group and a heck of a lot better than rejoicing in my supposed E.T. status. Can you give me some idea of what we're talking about here?"

Dave slid down on his spine and propped his feet on the coffee table. "Okay, let's start with a definition—one I don't necessarily buy into but that is accepted by UFO buffs. There are Wanderers. This is where you come in, so listen up. Wanderers are extraterrestrial souls who have agreed to be born in human bodies and only gradually come to realize their true identity."

Christy choked on a sudden indrawn breath. "As they bloom?" she asked in a cracked voice.

"So to speak." Dave beamed at her, a teacher to a brilliant student. "They bloom."

"And I'm supposed to be one of them?" She stood up and paced around the room, stopping to look at him in exasperation. "It's crazy. The most ridiculous thing I've ever heard."

"Hey, don't kill the messenger. You asked, I'm telling. Look at it this way, you're in good company. Ben Franklin and Thomas Jefferson were no slouches."

"I think I have a headache." Christy sank back

into the cushions and closed her eyes. Her lids had barely lowered when they flew open. "Exactly what does Aunt Tillie expect me to do?"

"Relax. You don't have to re-write the Constitution. She thinks you're perfect just as you are. And—" he dipped his head in a gallant nod "—I agree."

"Thanks." She gave him a glum look. "But I know she expects something. At the very least, for me to drag home an alien, marry him and produce pointy-eared little great grand nieces and nephews."

"You're mixing Mr. Spock into the equation," he said dryly. "Tillie is simply convinced that your presence on this planet will somehow uplift the human condition. After all, that's what Wanderers do."

"*Simply?* That's *all* I'm supposed to do?" Christy stared at him, stunned. "Make the world a better place?"

"Right." Dave nodded. "But not all at once, you know. One person at a time is just fine with Tillie."

"That's real big of her." Reaching for her glass, she gazed down at the tea as if it were a crystal ball. Finally, looking at the man across from her, she murmured, "Why on earth does she think I could do such a thing."

Dave sat up, resting his elbows on his thighs, studying her. "Well, you know your aunt better than I do, but in this last month, getting ready for this trip, I learned something about her—she's a clearsighted idealist. She sees right into the heart of a person. Sees what we are capable of being and doing. I'll tell you, it's pretty humbling."

"And scary."

"Yeah, that too."

"But—"

He held up a hand to stop her. "What she sees in you is an extraordinary ability to love and nurture, so extraordinary that it's proof to her of your unearthly nature. Of course, she had a head start in her belief, with your old soul and all." He grinned again when Christy rolled her eyes.

"But everyone can—"

"No, they can't," he said gently. "You have the knack, according to Tillie. You've done it all your life, with friends, relatives and perfect strangers. And in the last few years, you've taken three men who were well on their way to becoming entrepreneurial robots and humanized them."

"The three exes? Right." Christy took another swig of tea. "I did a great job. So great that I had to break all three engagements. For some reason, I seem to be attracted to the hardheaded types. No, make that past tense. I've reformed."

Dave shook his head, refusing to be distracted. "From what Tillie says, you were wise enough to know you needed more than they could give, but you taught them enough about love so they could find it and cherish it in some other woman."

"*That's* proof that I'm an alien? Give me a break, Dave. I've never heard such—"

"And look what's happened since you've joined the caravan."

"What, for heaven's sake?"

"You've molded us into a group," he said simply.

"No way." Christy shook her head, frowning at him. "You were that already."

"Nope. We were a bunch of individuals, each

with our own agenda. You're a born peacemaker, Christy, whether you know it or not." He eyed her thoughtfully. "You have a way of bringing out the good in us that Tillie so clearly sees."

Touched and troubled by his words, Christy couldn't think of a thing to say.

Dave had no such problem. Chuckling, he said, "You're never going to change Tillie's mind, you know. So my advice, if you're open to it, is to live your life as you damn well please. Tillie will find something to confirm her belief in whatever you do."

Tillie *wouldn't* change her mind, Christy reflected as she pedaled up the dusty road to Shane's house. After all, didn't she still absolutely believe Brandy was married to an alien? Of course she did. And all because of a misunderstanding that had to do with his birthday or sun sign or something equally weird. Bringing an E.T. into the family had rated right at the peak of Tillie's list of lifetime achievements. The only way she could top that would be to produce one from the family tree.

Shuddering at the thought, Christy dismounted at the top of the hill, puffing, and looked out over Shane's land. The shortcut he had pointed out was steep but cut almost a mile off her original route.

The curving black ribbon of highway that ran through his property neatly bisected the lush, green grass along the river from the sere slopes dotted with tumbleweeds, Mormon Tea, small cactus and sagebrush. Absorbed in the staggering contrast between the two sides, Christy jumped when Shane's voice broke the silence.

"Hard to believe, isn't it?"

Turning, just as he effortlessly swung off Milt and stepped forward to join her, she tamped down a flicker of appreciation and an almost claustrophobic need to back away. He removed his Stetson, towering a good eight inches over her five-foot-seven-inch frame. The breadth of his shoulders made her deeply aware of her femininity, of a body that seemed fragile compared to his sinew and muscle. It was a new thought for someone who had always considered her slim form sturdy enough to deal with any situation.

"How on earth did you get behind me?" she demanded.

He shook his head, apparently pitying the poor tenderfoot. "Hell, I could have been moving my herd back here and you wouldn't have heard me. You were too engrossed in what's down there." Shane gestured to the panoramic view before them. "Can't say I blame you. It's a hell of a view. It affects me the same way. Every time I look at it, I think of itchy feet, dumb luck and persistence."

"How touching," Christy said dryly. She gave Milt a wary glance as he ambled closer. "You *are* going to explain that, aren't you?"

Shane tucked his sunglasses in his shirt pocket and wiped his forehead with the arm of his shirt. "My great-grandfather came west with a couple of friends, looking for ranch land. The farther they came, the drier it got. The other two wanted to stop around what's now Las Vegas, but he wasn't ready to settle yet. He told them he wanted to look around for a while and took off on his horse. About five days later, he reached the other side of that hill.'' Shane pointed to a crag dotted with cactus and sagebrush. "It was dark, so he made camp and fell asleep. The next morning, he walked to the top of the hill and looked down on the river and grassland."

Christy nodded. "That takes care of the first two, what about the persistence?" She jumped when Milt snorted and nuzzled her hair.

"He marked off the land he wanted and went back for his friends. They all bought land and spent the rest of their lives making the ranches pay."

"And I'd guess that each succeeding generation has done the same." Her gaze brushed over his determined, cleft chin and full, firm lips, drifted past his straight nose and stopped, stunned once again by his eyes. Black as his pupil, they should have been flat, lifeless. Instead, they were liquid with expression, alive with an emotion that sent a tug of anxiety down her spine. "And it looks like they've done very well," she added breathlessly, turning away.

Looking out at the sere landscape, he shook his head. "Not in everything. We've all tried to find water over there, but so far we haven't hit the right place."

Christy shifted restlessly when Milt lipped a few strands of her hair. "Do you know it's there? For sure?"

"Hell no. But the old man was an optimist. When he bought the land, he took plenty so he could expand. And that's exactly what I intend to do—when I find water."

Christy cleared her throat. "That sort of ties in to the reason for my visit today."

Frowning down at her bicycle, Shane said, "I've been meaning to talk to you about that."

"My visit?"

Shane sighed. "No, the bicycle. Why don't I leave a horse for you. It would make your rides to the ranch a hell of a lot easier."

For you maybe, Christy thought, moving again when Milt nuzzled her cheek. "Thanks, but no. I need the exercise." Patting the handlebars of her bike, she said, "And I don't have to feed, water or brush this. And I don't have to step around smelly calling cards. Besides," she finished, moving to the other side of Shane, "I'm not all that comfortable around horses."

He looked from Milt to her wary expression. "You're afraid of Milt here?"

Frowning at him, she said, "I didn't say I was afraid. Exactly. I just have a healthy sense of self-preservation."

"Milt is a big softy. He wouldn't hurt you."

Christy sighed. "Milt is huge, is what he is. He has big teeth, which at the moment are getting awfully close to my ear. He also has big feet. So, since I don't particularly like to be chewed or stepped on, I prefer to keep my distance." Milt apparently didn't feel the same way, because he kept crowding her until she was pressed against Shane's long body.

Darting a suspicious glance at him, Christy demanded, "Did you teach him to do this?"

With an innocent look she didn't believe for a minute, Shane wrapped his hands around her waist and lifted her away from the curious horse. Holding her wrist in a light grip, he said, "Nope, I don't have the time or patience. He just likes women. The way they smell."

"I don't wear perfume."

"You don't have to." Shane bent his head and sniffed, his nostrils flaring as he caught her delicate scent. "Your shampoo smells like strawberries. Milt likes strawberries." He dropped a whisper of a kiss in the sensitive area behind her ear lobe, smiling when her pulse jolted beneath his thumb. "So do I."

Dazed for a moment by the sensation of his warm breath brushing her ear, Christy leaned into him. The man was good, she thought with a hazy sigh as his arm slid around her waist and tugged her closer. Very good. He was— The feel of her heart thudding against his chest shocked her into moving. Stiffening, she pushed away, stopping only when she was out of reach. The man was damned *dangerous,* and way too hard to handle, that's what he was.

Giving him a searing glance, Christy watched as he smiled and slid his big hands in his back pockets. Rattled both by his touch and her reaction, she opted to ignore the entire situation. "Earlier, you were talking about finding water?"

Shane nodded.

"That's the reason I was going to your place. Ruth Ann wants to know if she can take a group over there," Christy nodded toward the desert on the far side of the road, "and do some dowsing. She promises that they'll do no damage."

Shane shrugged. "How can they hurt cactus and

dry dirt? Sure, if they want to play, tell them to feel free. After all, they are my guests.''

Christy's brows rose at his tolerant tone. If one were inclined to think that way, it could almost be considered patronizing, she reflected. "You don't believe in dowsing?''

Alerted by the coolness of the question, and knowing her bond with the seniors, he weighed his words before answering. "Let's put it this way, I've never known anyone to do it successfully. I know some people who swear by it, but I'm inclined to think it's right up there with myth and folklore.''

"I see. How do *you* go about finding water?''

"Hiring a hydrologist who has several degrees stuffed in his back pocket.''

"Ah.'' Christy thought of Ruth Ann and the group of amateurs who were anticipating the adventure of learning and trying a new skill. Shane was probably right, she thought, but then Ruth Ann just might have a couple of aces up her sleeve.

"Ah, what?''

"Nothing. Really. I was just thinking that your professionals haven't done such a hot job.''

"It's hard to find something if it isn't there.'' Shane lifted a hand to her hair, tucking a strand behind her ear. "Are you coming to the house for dinner tonight?''

Nodding, Christy reached for her bike. "You bet. I'd walk barefoot through your prime piece of desert for one of Ben's meals.''

"Will you stay and visit awhile after the others leave? I'll take you home later.'' He watched her expressive face, reading her doubts as clearly as if she had shouted them.

"Shane, I don't think—"

"Don't think. Just stay. Please?"

Knowing she'd regret it, knowing she was asking for trouble, she gave a reluctant nod. "I'll stay."

Chapter Four

Christy put aside her magazine and glanced from her watch to her aunt's avid expression as she poured over a market tabloid with headlines screaming about UFO abductions. "Don't you think we should leave now?"

They sat in the motor home, protected from the numbing chill that enveloped the area. Heavy clouds had swept in during the night, catching the weather bureau by surprise. The storm Tillie had mentioned was building up steam. Lashing winds bent the trees and torrents of rain had formed a lake that would soon be lapping at the tires of the motor homes.

Nodding, Tillie cast a last yearning glance at the photos accompanying the article. "The others said they would be ready about now, and Shane will be worried if we don't arrive soon."

She was right.

Shane stepped out on his front porch and scanned

the road leading to the house. Only the overhanging eaves protected him from the drumming rain as he braced his hands on the wide porch rail and narrowed his eyes. "They should be here by now. Damn it, I don't like it. You know how boggy that area gets in bad weather."

Hank followed him out, slamming the screen door behind him. "Ben said they'd be here about ten. It's still early."

Shane grunted, keeping his eyes on the road. "Tell that to the rain." Turning, he scowled at his foreman. "And that's another thing. How did it get here? There wasn't a thing, not one damned thing, about a storm on the weather channel last night."

Shrugging, Hank took another quick look at the road. "Don't blame me. The only time I heard about it was a couple of days ago when the old lady mentioned it."

He paused, remembering what Shane had told him the night before, then cleared his throat. "You know I don't place much stock in this psychic stuff, but I've been thinkin' on something she said and I thought you ought to know."

Shane looked over his shoulder at the older man, bracing himself. It was getting to be a knee-jerk reaction whenever Tillie was mentioned, he reflected. It had been said a time or two that he had a serious issue with control, but damn it, it *was* his ranch. Where she was concerned, he didn't know what to expect, and he didn't like waiting for the other shoe to fall. "What is it?"

"Well, first, there's this guy, Walter, who seems

to know a helluva lot about the ranch. More than he should, to my way of thinking.''

"Yeah, I know about him.'' The talkative dead husband. "He's okay.'' He thought.

"He mentioned the cattle." Hank snorted. "Calls 'em cows."

"Yeah."

"Seems he don't like the idea of them in the hollow."

"Yeah."

"Then the old lady asked me how long it would take to move the herd down there, and I said a few hours 'cause they weren't very far away."

"Yeah? Then what?"

"She just thought real hard and said that this morning would be okay."

The two men looked at each other. Skepticism, doubt and uneasiness vibrated between them on the rain-drenched porch.

Rolling his shoulders to relieve the growing tension, Shane gazed at the road again. "So what are you saying?"

"That maybe the crazy little lady ain't really so crazy. That maybe she sent Ben up here to cook and stayed there on purpose until the storm came—"

"So I couldn't put the herd down there until after it rained?"

Thoughtful, Hank gave a deliberate nod. "Yeah, that's what I was thinking. More or less."

The muted rumble of engines broke through the pounding rain, galvanizing the two of them.

Hank reached for the door. "I'll get my slicker and the Jeep and lead them to the cabin."

"Okay. Show them where to hook up. I'll follow with the van, so they can pile in and come back to the house."

With his hand on the knob, Hank half turned to stare at him. "You're letting them stay in the house?"

Shane nodded, his expression grim. "During the day. While it's raining. Let's just say I want them where I can keep my eyes on them."

Shane stepped out on the porch that evening, catching the screen door before it slammed. His nostrils flared as he approached Christy, appreciating the delicate fragrance of strawberry shampoo and night air softened by the raging storm. The rain gauge indicated that six inches had fallen before the tempest had dissipated as suddenly as it had blown in.

Easing down beside Christy on the swing, he set it in motion with a prod from his booted foot. "Are they always like that?"

She looked up with a wry smile. "Who? Tillie and the seniors? Yep. At least in the few days that I've known them. They all have something to say, and it's usually at the top of their lungs." Easing away from him until she was pressed against the armrest, she tucked a foot beneath her, studying Shane. He seemed surprisingly relaxed after a day with her aunt's crew.

"And are you always the peacemaker?"

Christy tilted her head, considering the question. "I don't know. I don't see myself that way at all." Leaning back, she wondered if he and Dave were right.

"It looked pretty obvious to me." He draped his arm along the back of the swing, cupping her shoulder with his hand. "You waded right in the middle of them and had them eating out of your hand in less than five minutes. They also compromised on a trip to Rachel tomorrow instead of pushing for their favorite screwy plan to take on an armed force. I'd say that was definitely the work of a peacemaker."

Black misty clouds swept east, driven by the wind. Night sounds built in the aftermath of the deluge, surrounding them. Crickets gradually resumed their busy chirping, and in the distance the ululant cry of a coyote signaled its location.

Shane abruptly broke the silence. "She knew, didn't she?"

Giving the question the consideration it deserved, she finally nodded. "That the hollow would be flooded in the storm? Probably."

"Probably?"

Aware of his frustration, Christy nodded again. "That's the best I can do. I don't know what goes on in her head or her psyche. All I can tell you is that there's usually a reason for whatever Aunt Tillie does. She definitely marches to the sound of her own drummer. When people don't respond to her hints, she simply handles the situation in her own inimitable way."

Shane swore with feeling. "There has *never* been a flash flood down there. She probably saved me a couple dozen head of cattle."

"Good." She resisted the urge to pat his arm. "I'm glad we didn't stay there for nothing, worrying about the batteries in the RV. At least, *I* worried.

Everyone else knew we were equipped with generators." She slid a curious look at him. "Didn't you know it could be dangerous to have the cattle there?"

He gave a shrug. "Sure, things like that are always possible, but in the history of the ranch, we've never had a rain that sudden and hard—so I wouldn't have thought twice about putting them there. If they'd been there when a storm rolled in, I would have checked on them." He brooded silently for a moment. "But this time, I couldn't have pulled them out in time."

She shouldn't be here, she thought a moment later, moving restlessly in the sudden charged silence. It had been crazy to stay after the seniors had returned to their motor homes the past two nights. Shane had been the perfect host both times, driving her back in his Jeep when she'd asked, but the tension flickering between them since that first day on the hill had grown to a palpable force. And he couldn't hide the heat and hunger in his black eyes.

She had been wrong. Dead wrong. Constant exposure to Shane would not make her immune to him. Nor would it create an alpha-male shield, protecting her from the impact he had on her nerve endings. No, she had been playing with fire and she knew, as he turned slowly to face her, that she was about to get burned.

Slipping to her feet, she started across the porch. "I think I'd better get back—"

"Christy, wait. We need to talk." Shane caught up with her and dropped a hand on her shoulder, turning her to face him, keeping her there with a hold both gentle and implacable. "About us."

"I said it before and I meant it, Shane. There is no us." Keeping her voice steady was an act that took all of her will.

Shane didn't give her a chance to argue. His hands slid to her waist and he lifted, settling her on the porch rail. In the next instant he stepped between her thighs, keeping them open. Looking down, he took in her stubborn expression. "Saying it doesn't make it true. You're wrong. You want me as much as I want you. Those green eyes of yours don't lie, honey. And they say out loud what I'm thinking every minute of the day."

Grabbing his shirt for support, she could feel the male heat of him beneath her hands, pouring through her fingers into her body with every beat of his heart. He was too close, too big, too male, too...everything. Everything that threatened her.

"It's the wrong time," she whispered, caught in the spell of heat and want.

"It's the only time we have. Right now. Tonight. Tomorrow. Less than three weeks."

Three weeks. The words jarred her enough to stiffen her spine. "And just what do we have during that time? A hot affair?"

"I've learned to take what I can get in this life. And I give back every bit as much as I get." His black eyes never left her face. "There's nothing wrong with an affair, if both people are willing. And want it. And, baby, I want it, I want *you*. Bad. Look at me and tell me that you don't feel the same way."

Christy took a deep breath, struggling with need

as he tugged her closer. Of course she wanted him. She wasn't made of ice. She wanted him, she realized with stunning clarity, more than she had ever wanted any man. At any time. Any place. But she had one small kernel of sense left, one nugget of wisdom that reminded her the two of them were on a collision course. An affair that would end in three weeks was not her idea of a relationship. And while she had survived three broken engagements in the past two years, she knew with absolute certainty that she wouldn't walk away from an affair with Shane unscathed.

Feeling her beaded nipples stabbing Shane's chest, she caught her breath and pulled back. His hands tightened on her shoulders, steadying her.

He slid his thumbs under her chin, turning her face up, until her mouth was just a breath away. Dipping his head, he brushed his lips over hers, groaning at what her warm sweetness was doing to his body. His muscles clenched when Christy sighed against his mouth, blending their breath. Moving his hands, he ran his fingers through her hair, flexing them against her scalp, holding her still as he dragged his lips across hers to kiss the corner of her mouth.

"Sweet," he muttered. "So damned sweet."

Gasping for air, Christy put her palms against his broad shoulders and pressed. She felt him hesitate. "Shane, stop. This won't work. I need to think."

"That's the last thing you need to do," he muttered, lifting his head and looking down at her with impatient yearning.

She waited for him to back off, knowing she had no leverage. If he stepped away, it would be because he was willing to move, not because she had the strength to make him.

When he didn't budge, she sighed and ran a hand through her tumbled hair. Still holding him off with her other hand, Christy looked up at him, wincing at his stubborn expression. Before he could say anything, she made a lightning review of her options and decided it was time for the truth. All of it.

"Look, right before I joined Aunt Tillie and friends, I broke up with my fiancé. He was a stubborn, aggressive man. A lot like you." He took a quick breath and she held up a hand to stop him.

"I broke up with him because he couldn't give me what I wanted."

"What, money?" The two words came up from somewhere deep within him, his voice stark.

Her eyes glittering with sudden fury, Christy smacked his chest with the sides of her fists. "*Money?* Get away from me, you blockhead. And let...me...*down.*" It only added to her rage when he lifted her as if she weighed no more than a leaf, and let her slide down his frame, making sure she felt every inch of his aroused body.

As soon as her feet touched the ground, she swung away from him, only stopping when she found herself behind a wicker rocking chair. Keeping it between them, she glared at him.

"Money? I make my own, thank you. I'm a damn good freelance writer and I make all that I need. No one else pays my way."

"Then what?" he demanded, barely concealing his self-disgust. His careless words had incited the very situation he'd been avoiding, and he could see the barrier between them getting higher every second. "What couldn't he give you?"

"*Love!* That's what." Her sharp glance told him even an idiot would know that.

The adrenaline that had swept through her system with such satisfying fury left just as swiftly. Sliding into the rocker with an exhausted gesture, she narrowed her eyes and pinned him with a look that informed him it wouldn't take much to pump her up again.

"Right now, my focus is on my career. I don't have time for the complication of a man in my life. If all goes well, I'll have an editorial position, probably in Los Angeles, at the end of the year. That's as far ahead as I can think."

Still far from forgiving him, she scowled. "So why did you think I wanted money?"

Shane frowned down at her, no happier than she was. "Two women, two lies, babe," he said succinctly. "Both said they loved me and made plans for a marriage, a life together. Both times I found out what they wanted was money."

And you were hurt. "Don't call me babe," she said automatically.

He continued as if she hadn't spoken. "Instead, they walked away with whatever gifts I had given them. It was worth it, though, for the lesson I learned."

"And that was?"

"Not to expect career women to stick around for the long run."

His expressionless eyes made her heart ache. He had probably been much younger, she thought, an age when young, idealistic men dreamed of finding the perfect woman. He had offered his heart, twice, and found it wasn't enough. No wonder he was bitter.

Christy thought briefly of the women, picturing soft, faceless bodies and greedy hearts. What fools. They'd had a treasure placed in their hands and hadn't had the sense to recognize it. He was a good man, she reflected. Honorable, with the type of steadfastness bred into him by generations of people who were rooted to the land.

But she wouldn't give him any more sympathy than he'd offered her. One glance was enough to realize that he wouldn't appreciate the gesture. Aside from that, it was dangerous. It could catapult them right back into each other's arms.

When he started toward her, she pointed a finger at him as if it were a cocked pistol. "Stay right there. I mean it, Shane. I'm at your ranch for one reason only—well, actually, two. To keep an eye on Aunt Tillie and write several articles about seniors traveling together. I've paid my dues in this field, and in a year I'm stepping on the next rung of the ladder."

Keeping her eyes on him to make sure he didn't move, Christy took a deep breath and slowly began to unwind. "This is important to me." She hesitated. "I majored in journalism. Writing is the only thing I ever wanted to do."

Shane nodded, understanding. "I feel the same way about ranching."

"I've written for every kind of magazine you can imagine, starting with crafts and local monthlies. I spent several years working on spec, sending out enough query letters to strip a forest. I did interviews up the wazoo.'' Her eyes kindled with an emotion he couldn't identify. ''And then, take the ecology magazine I worked for.''

His anger dissipated as suddenly as it had erupted, Shane raised his brows. ''Okay, let's take it.''

Remembering, she leaned back in the rocker. ''I loved that magazine, and the people. Worked there the past two years and did some of my best work. And you know what?'' Sitting up, she frowned at him, the fire back in her eyes.

Shane shook his head, wondering where the hell she was headed.

''I almost blew it with them. Three times. You know why?''

Shane waited, knowing she was going to tell him—and that he wasn't going to like whatever she said.

''Men. That's why. Men a lot like you. Too much like you. They were strong, attractive, had a passion for their work that I found fascinating. They wanted me, and I fell for them. All the way. And we got engaged.''

Alert now, Shane straightened. ''Three men? In two years?''

''Don't go there, McBride.'' Christy, on a roll now, narrowed her eyes in warning. ''I heard enough about that from my family. I broke it off with each and every one of them, and you know why?''

Shane lowered himself to the rail, knowing now exactly where she was heading.

Jumping to her feet, Christy paced in quick, nervous steps to the door and back. Swinging to face Shane, she filled her lungs with air and blew it out with an explosive sound. "Because none of them understood the first thing about love. They wanted me, enough to ask me to marry them. But did they love me?" She pierced him with a look and answered her own question. "No. They didn't know the meaning of the word, and I'll be damned if I walk into another relationship with a man just as thick. In fact, I'm not getting involved with *any* man, especially for a less-than-three-week affair.

"I finally figured it out after number three. They said they loved me, and I think they really believed they did. But you know what they really cared about? Their companies. Work was their number one priority. *Their* work. They never gave a thought to my job. Or realized that I was as dedicated to my career as they were to theirs."

Christy shrugged, remembering the lack of understanding, the disappointment on both sides.

"What happened?" His voice was quiet.

"Which time? Number one was launching his company's new computer at a big formal affair. He couldn't understand why I was in Montana writing about people who were losing their ranches because noxious weeds had invaded their grazing land, crowding out the vegetation and killing their cattle.

"Number two got upset when I wouldn't stay and celebrate a huge new contract with the CEO and wife of the other company. I was in the middle of the ocean with Greenpeace, confronting a fishing vessel whose crew made a practice of using dolphins for target practice with their semiautomatics."

Sighing, she tucked her hands in the pockets of her jeans and contemplated the pointed toes of her boots. "Number three? I was in the redwoods with a team of U.S. geological survey ecologists testing controlled burns. Doesn't really matter what he was up to. I wasn't there—at any of the functions. But you know what? I almost passed on each of those assignments so I *would* be there."

"But you didn't."

She lifted her gaze to his, a flash of anger darkening her eyes. "Damn straight I didn't. But I was tempted—and feeling guilty. I thought I should be with them, to support them. They thought so, too."

And that had been the breaking point, she reflected. Not one of them had seen the importance of her job. Not one had asked about her articles. Not one of them had understood.

"So that was it?" Shane kept his voice level, wanting to hear the rest. "You opted out?"

Christy nodded. "Yeah. With each of them. We discussed it, realized it wouldn't work." And that had to be the understatement of the year, she thought wryly, remembering their astonishment and lack of understanding.

"Did they make it easy for you?"

"Hardly." She closed her eyes a moment, remembering the endless telephone calls after each breakup. "But I know what I can give to a man, and I finally realized that it shouldn't be a one-way street. I wasn't going to spend the rest of my life beating my head against a stone wall. Each time, I told myself it was a different man, a different situation, but it ended the same way. I wasn't a fast learner, but I finally got the message."

"And that was?"

Good question. The man did have a way with words. In the past months, she had lived with regret, the certainty that she had been right, a deep sense of caution and the knowledge that she wouldn't rush into the arms of another man—no matter what. And that she would wait forever for the right man.

"It was a simple one." She looked up, blinking at the barely leashed hunger in his dark eyes. "That I won't get involved with another man unless he can love me as much as I'll love him."

Turning to lean her arms on the rail across the stairs from Shane, Christy gazed at the clearing sky, losing herself in the peacefulness of the glittering stars.

"Why'd you leave the ecology magazine?"

She gave a small shrug and half turned toward him. "It wasn't my idea. It was part of a conglomerate taken over by a big media consortium. The new parent company already had a similar magazine, so they merged the two staffs and I lost out to a feature writer with more seniority. But they liked my writing and hooked me up with a travel magazine."

"It doesn't sound as satisfying."

"It's not, but they sweetened the pot when they said there would be editorial positions open in several magazines next year, and I'd have a good chance at one of them." Turning back to her contemplation of the stars, she tried to convince herself that she was satisfied, fulfilled.

"I want you, Christy."

Slowly, she turned to face him, thinking she had misunderstood. One look at his determined gaze told her she hadn't. Fisting her hands on her hips, she sent him a look that should have sizzled his eyelashes. "Have I been talking to myself here? Didn't you hear a word I said?"

He nodded. "Every one of them. I just don't see how they apply to us. Neither of us is looking for a permanent arrangement." One lithe movement brought him next to her. She blinked in astonishment when he slowly lifted her hand to his mouth. Pressing a kiss in her palm and closing her fingers over it, he sighed. "We could be good together, sweetheart. Better than you can imagine."

Taking a shaky breath, Christy pressed her free hand against his chest and shook her head. "Don't do this to me, Shane. I seem to be more vulnerable than I thought, and, damn it, I don't want you."

"Liar." He brushed his lips across her knuckles, never taking his eyes from her face. Satisfaction surged through him when the pulse in her throat fluttered like a wild bird.

Stepping back, she found herself sandwiched between his hard body and the fence rail. His heat and the clean, soap-and-water male scent of him jangled her senses, made her realize just how susceptible she was to him. "Well, I don't *want* to want you," she said breathlessly.

"That's not the same thing at all."

Rattled by the obstinate determination gleaming in his dark eyes, she tried again. "What I mean is, my body wants you, but my head knows it shouldn't."

She stopped, scowling when her mind caught up with her words.

Shane gave a sharp groan and dropped her hand. "That'll help me get a good night's sleep," he muttered, his gaze hungrily taking in her parted lips, flustered eyes and tumbling hair that would look just fine spread on his pillow. "I'll think about that tonight when—" A trill from his shirt pocket cut off his words.

Swearing, he pulled the phone from his pocket. "This better be damned good," he snarled.

"Oh, dear." Tillie's startled voice sounded in his ear. "I don't know if it is or not."

"Tillie? How'd you get this number?"

"I don't know, Shane, dear. I just poke at numbers."

"This number is unlisted."

"Oh? I don't understand why people get telephones if they don't want to talk to anyone. Do you?"

One sharp glance at Christy told him that she had regained her composure. Regret caused him to miss Tillie's next words. "I'm sorry, what did you say?"

"Nothing important, dear. Only that you startled me so, I forgot why I called. Goodbye."

His gaze was steady on Christy's face as he lowered the phone. "She hung up."

"What did she want?"

"I don't know. She forgot." Watching amusement lighten her eyes, he said, "Does she do that often?"

Smiling, Christy shrugged. "Let's just say she has an impeccable sense of timing. And speaking of time, it's getting late. I'd better leave."

Shane looked down at her with narrowed eyes for a long moment. "I'll drive you back. The ground is still too wet to walk."

The drive was quick and filled with silence.

She was a paradox, Shane brooded. She owned comfortably worn cowboy boots but practically hyperventilated if a horse got close. She was made to fit a man's hands and mouth, and she had No Trespassing signs posted all around her. She had enough love for an eternity and was afraid to share it. It wasn't as if he wanted it all, or even a part of it, forever. Three lousy weeks, that's what he wanted.

When he braked to a stop, Christy slid out and softly closed the door, waiting until he drove away. As she stepped between two motor homes, she heard Tillie chatting with Ruth Ann. At the mention of her own name, she stopped, tilting her head to hear better, not even debating the merits of listening to a private conversation. Where Tillie was involved, she needed every advantage she could get.

"I'm so glad you sent a call out over the Net," Ruth Ann said. "It's going to be a good trip. For everyone. Maybe even Christy."

Edging forward to peer around the motor home, Christy saw her aunt give a definite nod.

"Yes. Christy will…" Tillie lapsed into thought.

Ruth Ann smiled at the older woman. "Will what?"

"I think…yes…she will find her soul mate."

Sighing at the thought, Ruth Ann's smile was dreamy. "Do you know who he is?"

Tillie gazed out at the star-laden sky. "Oh yes. The one who will give her a piece of the universe."

Chapter Five

Christy looked up at Shane from the seat beside him in the crowded van. Twelve hours had passed since he'd left her, and she was heavy-eyed from a sleepless night. Memories of his rock-hard body against hers and his determined *I want you* had haunted the dark hours. And Aunt Tillie's latest revelation to Ruth Ann hadn't helped, either. "Are you sure you can spare the time for this trip?"

He gave a brief nod. "Yeah, I'm fine. You know, if anyone had told me last week that I'd be doing this, I'd have said they were nuts."

"How would you define 'this?'" Keep it light, she reminded herself.

"How about driving UFO believers down the highway skirting an Air Force base where it's rumored, by people like the ones in this van, that the government is hiding alien spacecraft?" he asked dryly, slanting a considering look at her. "All in all, I've just about decided that *I'm* nuts."

And I'm not far behind, Christy reflected. All twelve of them were crammed in Shane's large van, heading northwest on Highway 375. The road had been renamed the Extraterrestrial Highway and boasted several large green signs, showing a saucer with red and yellow lights, planted along the road to prove it.

That the highway had been renamed in an effort to promote tourism was not up for debate. In a state that had Las Vegas, with its pyramids and exploding volcanoes, this was nothing new. That Tillie's group was actually going to Rachel, population about thirty and self-described center of alien activity, was a testament to her aunt's persistence in the face of reason and logic.

"We're on the edge of great discoveries," Tillie sighed.

Shane winced as her comment drifted up from behind him. "We're on the edge of insanity," he murmured.

Dave lifted his voice in warning. "Remember, guys, we're just going for lunch and to collect information."

Melinda tucked a strand of her shoulder-length, highlighted blond hair behind her ear and fished a coin out of her T-shirt pocket. "Tails says we head out to Area 51 before lunch, heads, we do it after."

"Hey, Rills, that's not on the agenda today. Besides, how do we know that isn't a two-headed quarter? I don't bet until I check it." Jack snagged the spinning coin out of the air and lost it just as quickly when Melinda plucked it from his open palm.

"Cops," she muttered, slipping the coin in the

pocket over her breast and patting it. "What's with you guys, Beatty? You're cynical, distrusting and always thinking the worst."

"Hey, what can I say? It's part of the oath we take."

"Don't mind him, Melinda." Opal directed a patient glance at Jack. "He's not as tough as he acts."

"Don't spread that around. I've got an image to protect." Leaning back, he dipped the bill of his baseball cap a bit lower over long salt-and-pepper hair, a small smile curving his lips. Nudging Melinda gently with his elbow, he said, "Nice shirt you got there, Rills."

"Thanks." She looked down at the bright red shirt picturing an alien waving to a human, with Long Time No See written below. With the exception of Christy and Shane, everyone in the van wore one that was identical.

"Coming up on Rachel pretty soon," Shane called out. Five minutes later he pulled into the dirt parking lot beside a one-story, rectangular building.

The seniors stepped out of the van, their expressions ranging from appreciation to amusement.

"I already like these people," Jim Sturgiss declared, his comprehensive glance taking in the plain white building with the bright sign. "Of course, since I retired from the Air Force, I like almost anyone who doesn't wear a uniform and has a sense of humor."

"Well, I don't know about their clothes, but they're sure up-front about their beliefs," Claude said, appreciatively eyeing the sign by the door. It pictured a big-eyed alien, and declared that earth-lings were welcome at the Little A'Le'Inn.

Shane looked at Christy and shook his head, grin-ning when she automatically hauled out her camera and started shooting.

"If this sign is any indication of what's inside, I can't wait," she muttered, getting a shot of several seniors reading the colorful sign.

The low-maintenance appearance of the interior of the combined restaurant and bar appeared to dazzle Tillie. After eyeing a bumper sticker that declared the car's driver braked for UFOs, she hiked up her long purple skirt and drifted toward a wall covered with a map of Area 51.

While the other seniors were greeted with enthu-siasm, Christy kept her eye on Tillie. Shane shifted his attention from one to the other. After studying the map, Tillie looked around, reached for a wooden chair and pulled it beside her. Before Shane could offer his help, she stepped up on the seat and leaned closer to the map, peering at the smaller print. It wasn't long before she reached up and placed her small hand over the Groom Lake area.

"What's she doing?" Shane muttered.

Christy kept her eyes on her aunt. "I don't know. I *never* know. But the area covered by her hand is supposed to be the center of all the shenanigans around here."

"So I've heard."

Preoccupied with Tillie's curious behavior, she nodded. "Really?"

"Yeah, really." His exasperation came through

loud and clear. "Honey, I've lived here all my life, remember?"

Christy blinked. Honey?

"I grew up on these stories. If anything unusual happens, it's big news around here. It makes all the radio talk shows, local TV and the papers. People around here are either believers or they learn to shut it out."

"And you shut it out." It wasn't a question. Honey? she thought again.

"You bet I did."

Just then, Tillie spun around and looked at them, wide-eyed with astonishment, almost vibrating with excitement.

"Ready to get down?" At her quick nod, Shane wrapped his large hands around her waist and gently lowered her until her toes touched the floor. "Are you all right?"

"Fine," she almost stuttered. "I just never expected...I've waited so—" She paused, anticipation bright in her blue eyes. "I wonder when he'll come?"

"Who?"

Tillie fiddled with her fluorescent green suspenders. "Well, Walter...."

"*Walter?*" Christy stared in horror at her aunt. "He's coming? *Here?*"

Once, after a visit with Tillie, she had written a list of things she hoped she would never experience. Heading the list was meeting Uncle Walter in the flesh.

"I thought you said he would never come back.

Here. On this plane…or cycle or whatever you call it.''

Tillie did a quick, joyous spin on her toes. ''It's true,'' she said when she settled down. ''I think. But I never expected to see…I always hoped, of course, but now it's actually…''

Attracted by the activity, Ben ambled over. ''What's going on?''

''Walter's coming to visit.'' Christy's harried glance turned to one of exasperation when he let out a whoop that brought the others.

''We're finally going to meet the mystery man.'' Ben made the announcement with a flourish worthy of a caped magician. ''Walter's dropping in on us.'' Turning to Tillie, he asked, ''What should I make for dinner?''

''Dinner?''

''For Walter.''

When Tillie turned her baffled gaze on him, he looked around at the others. ''He *does* eat, doesn't he?''

''But, that's not—''

Eyes narrowed on her in concern, Shane saw that Tillie's response was lost in the din created by her vociferous friends. Finally, she shook her head and sighed, slipping away to study a rack of videos.

When he turned to follow the small woman whose open-armed embrace of life touched something deep within him, Christy laid her hand on his arm, bringing him to a halt. ''I think she needs to be alone for a while.'' Her fingers tightened at his dark, unconvinced gaze. ''She gets this way sometimes. It's as if she's on overload and needs to wind down.''

"I wonder why?" He scowled at the exuberant seniors. "I could use some downtime myself." Sending another glance at the quiet woman, he realized just how much he cared for her. He didn't understand her or the bizarre world she lived in, but damn it, he cared. He didn't want her hurt. "What do you think happened?"

Touched by his uneasiness, Christy tucked her arm through his. "I don't know. Maybe Uncle Walter placed his morning call. Maybe she felt something when she touched the map. Maybe the noise has tired her. All I can tell you is I've seen her like this before. She's working something out, and it'll take a few minutes. Trust me, she'll be okay."

"But look at her. She's staring at those weird alien videos and she doesn't even see them. Normally, she'd be turning cartwheels."

"I know." Christy bumped her hip against him and herded him toward a table. When they were seated, she handed him a menu. "I used to worry when she got quiet like that, but after it happened a couple of times I realized that she just goes inside to think."

"Inside?"

Refusing to be discouraged by the blank inquiry, she said, "You know, mulling. Brooding. *Thinking,* for heaven's sake. Everyone does it." Tapping the corner of his menu with hers, she nodded toward her aunt. "Look, she's coming out of it."

Tillie's gaze focused on one particular video, and she snapped it up, studying it with delight. Tucking it under her arm, she moved toward their table, stopping to pat Shane on the shoulder. "Dear boy. You worry so." Allowing her hand to linger there, she tilted her head, gazing at his denim shirt. As usual, the pocket was embroidered with a red swirl of stars. "Interesting," she murmured. "I wonder if you know you know what you know? I'll have to ask Walter."

Ignoring Shane's disconcerted expression, she dropped into the chair beside Christy. "I'll have a BLT."

Shane looked straight at her, a stubborn look in his black eyes. "I don't want you talking to Walter about me. If I know anything about anything, I'll let you know. And you haven't even seen the menu yet."

"So I haven't." Blue eyes glimmering with amusement, she picked up the menu and briefly scanned it. "I'll have a BLT. And lemonade."

The other seniors followed, pulling tables and chairs together and placing their orders. Half of them were urging Ben to whip up an elegant meal for Walter, the others demanding a barbecue when the door opened.

"Uh-oh." Jack tensed, his shoulder brushing Shane's.

"What?"

"Sorry," he muttered. "Knee-jerk reaction. The guy who just came in is as high as a kite. Could be peyote or mescaline. Hell, it could be anything sold on the street. Or he could just look weird."

The man closed the door behind him, remaining there while he removed his sunglasses. Tucking them in his shirt pocket, he gazed around the room. The abundance of dark brown hair neatly brushed back into a ponytail that fell halfway down his back more than compensated for his receding hairline. Tall, muscular, with glittering hazel eyes, he fairly vibrated with intensity.

"Ah." Radiant, Tillie clasped her hands to her chest. "He's here!"

Eleven pairs of eyes, expressions ranging from blatant curiosity to deep reserve, shifted toward the door.

"*That's* Walter?" Ruth Ann's whisper could be heard throughout the room. "I thought he'd be older."

Speechless, Christy shrugged. She remembered him as a slim, wand of a man, but there was no telling what this transition thing did to people.

Forgetting discretion, they all turned to stare at him, watching with fascination. The man's gaze fell on Tillie, and he strode through the maze of tables, coming to a stop beside her chair. His penetrating gaze boring into hers, he said, "Do you believe in communication with the dead?"

Tillie smiled at him, a mischievous gleam in her eyes. Reaching out to touch his arm, she said, "Dear boy, I do it all the time."

"Jeez," Jack moaned. "I swear to God, she has an antenna. These nuts find her wherever she goes." Surging up, he invited the newcomer to join them and encouraged the others to move down to make room. He pulled another chair over, sliding it between his and Shane's. In the confusion, he muttered to Shane, "We're the two biggest guys here. Tillie won't let him get away, and I don't want him by the women."

Shane nodded, waiting to sit until the man slid into the chair between them.

"My name is Aries," he announced, never removing his gaze from Tillie. "But most people call me Starman. I, too, speak with the dead."

While the others gazed at the man, mouths agape, Tillie gave him a blinding smile of encouragement.

Dave, on the other side of Shane, cleared his throat and leaned closer to whisper. "Probably talks to ants and gophers, too."

"Of course, they're not truly dead," Starman assured Tillie.

"Merely in transition," she agreed, giving him a serene nod of approval.

"One of them told me to come here today." His gold and green eyes glittered. "I have a message from the grays."

Grays? Shane's brows rose questioningly when he looked across the table at Christy.

Aliens, she mouthed, trying not to laugh.

Shane sighed and closed his eyes, wondering what else the weirdo next to him would do to brighten their day.

"They will visit you soon."

Tillie's cheeks were pink with excitement as she picked up a paper napkin to wipe perspiration from her frosty glass. Her hands shook, but her question was brief. "When?"

"Kinda takes the fun out of it," Dave murmured. "Being warned ahead of time, I mean."

"*Very* soon." Starman looked at them, his gaze focusing on each face like a laser. "You," he said in a portentous tone as he turned his attention back to Tillie, "are the worthy one."

Tillie blinked, disconcerted. "Oh, I'm sure the others are just as—"

The seniors could have been gnats for all the attention Starman gave them. "They're closer than you think," he told Tillie. "You came at the perfect time. It's almost as if you knew." He eyed her questioningly before he continued. "Right now, they have control of the phones. The static you hear when you pick up the receiver? That's them."

Tillie's eyes brightened. "It happened just this morning."

Shane turned toward Dave with a muffled groan. "It happens every damn time we have a storm."

"Why would they do that?" Melinda looked at Starman with more curiosity than belief.

"They have their reasons." He looked at her thoughtfully before admitting, "I don't really know. There's a lot they don't tell me. But they tap into our phone lines and listen to our conversations." Starman's intent gaze returned to Tillie.

"But, why?" Melinda persisted. "What's the point? What can they learn? I thought their intelligence was superior to ours."

"I think it's so they'll sound like us when they talk," Skip said. "You know, learn our idioms and all."

"There's even better news," Starman all but whispered, ignoring the comments. "They're here, all around us."

Dave leaned forward, drawn despite his skepticism. "Now?"

"Yes." Starman gave an energetic nod.

Skeptical as always, Jack looked over one shoulder then the other. "Then why can't we see them?"

"Good question." Starman's fingers tapped a frenetic tattoo on the table. "Because, when the they want to be, they're invisible."

"Oh, yeah, I knew that." Turning to the woman beside him, Jack demanded, "Didn't you know that, Rills?"

"I, uh, think I heard it somewhere." Amusement gleamed in her brown eyes, but her voice remained steady. "In fact, I'm positive I did."

"There, you see?" Jack looked back at Starman. "We're with you, partner."

"Most of us sense them at one time or another." Again, Starman's gaze touched each one. "Like when you feel someone looking over your shoulder, but you're in an empty room?"

Most of them nodded.

"That's them. They're watching to see if you're worthy."

Opal cleared her throat. "And if you are?"

"They become visible and visit you." After checking his watch, Starman shot to his feet. "Time to go. They only gave me a few minutes to deliver their message. I have to meet them. Now." Leaning across the table, he touched a finger to Tillie's cheek. "Remember," he murmured. "Worthy."

Turning, he paced through the tangle of tables and out the door, closing it softly behind him.

Jack stood, dropping his napkin on the table. "Excuse me a minute, I want a word with this guy." He followed the path Starman had taken, closing the door with a bang.

Returning sooner than they expected, he heard Opal's question as he headed for the tables. "*Was* that Walter?"

Melinda handed him his napkin, studying his expressionless face. "That was a short conversation."

"We didn't have one."

Patient, they waited. Finally Melinda sighed. "All right, I'll bite. Why not?"

"Because he wasn't there."

Nudging his hamburger closer to him, she gave him a sharp look. "Well, he did say he was in a hurry."

"So he did. I'd just like to know how he left."

Shane swallowed a bite of his ham sandwich. "What do you mean?"

"I mean I was out the door five seconds after he was, and he was gone. There's no dust in the parking lot from a moving car, and no car on the road. No one walking, either."

"Maybe he was on the other side of the building."

"I jogged around it." Jack put his untouched burger back on the plate. "Hell, I even checked the sky. Nothing."

As one, they turned toward Tillie. Regarding them in silence, she finally lifted her shoulders in a don't-ask-me shrug, stood and picked up her video. "Walter mentioned..." She paused, apparently thinking her way through a maze of possibilities. "But he said nothing at all about..." Leaving her words hanging, she pushed her chair back in and turned away to investigate the delights offered on the bookshelf against the wall.

"Does that mean Walter isn't coming?" Opal drooped in disappointment.

Dave ran a hand through his fair hair, leaving it standing in spikes. "Does she do that deliberately, just to drive us crazy?"

Not one of them had an answer.

Within an hour, loaded down with books, videos, postcards and alien souvenirs, they climbed back into the van. Once seated, Jack looked up from a booklet, marking his place with his finger. He had begun reading it in the bar, having a beer while the others browsed through the collection of available material.

After tapping Shane on the shoulder, he raised his voice, speaking over the conversations of those around him. "I have an idea. According to this map," he brandished the booklet, "we're going to pass a road that cuts into Groom Lake Road. That road, in turn, will take us to the entrance of the buffer zone of Area 51. I suggest, if Shane has time, that we drive over and take a look."

"Wait a minute." Dave's voice beat the others by about a half second. "No way. Some of us aren't in the mood to do time in whatever crummy jail they send people to around here."

Jack held up a hand to stem the flow of comments. "I said look, and that's all I meant. Swear to God, no busting in, nothing illegal."

Ruth Ann leaned forward to look at him. "Then why do it?"

"Just...to see exactly what we're up against."

Turning to look at those behind her, Christy admitted to herself that she was as curious as the seniors. "I can't see any harm in just looking."

Jack checked to see how the others felt. When each nodded in turn, he met Shane's gaze in the rearview mirror. "Then it's decided. If our host has time for the side trip, we go."

Shane's sigh could be heard all the way in the back seat. "I know the road. As long as we're this close, we might as well." Looking down at Christy, he muttered, "As I said earlier, I figure I'm nuts."

"What will Hank say?" She bit back a smile when he winced.

"I don't plan on telling him."

Jack flipped through the pages of the booklet and raised his voice. "Listen up. I want to read something about what we're getting into."

Christy settled back, listening to the litany of deterrents the government had on their side. Her research had acquainted her with most of them. Most of the others, whether from TV shows and documentaries or UFO newsletters, were also familiar with the information.

When they arrived, Christy followed the others out of the van, reflecting that the area looked amazingly benign. There were no tall gates, no armed sentries, no snarling Dobermans spewing trails of saliva their way. There was just more heat and desert, with the usual cover of chaparral and the occasional Joshua tree.

Shane, standing with Jack, watched Christy ready her camera as the others edged forward to read the chilling message on the warning signs. ''Would you have really led them into the restricted area?''

Snorting, Jack tilted his head toward the top of a nearby hill where a white Jeep Cherokee slid into view. Two men got out of the car and stood looking through binoculars at the crowd below. ''Hell, no. With the road sensors they've got, they knew we were coming while we were still several miles back. You might be lucky enough to get through for a while, but they'd find you in no time at all. That's a guaranteed fact, my friend.''

''Then why all the meetings, all the plans?''

Jack shrugged, grinning. ''At first, it was just fun. Actually, some of the ideas they came up with weren't half bad. With a little training, they'd make a great SWAT team. Anyway, I kept pushing the envelope, hoping they'd back down when they realized what they were up against.''

''But they didn't?''

Taking off his cap and wiping his forehead, Jack kept his gaze on the men above them. ''Not as of last night.''

''So you wouldn't help them break the law?''

''I'm a cop.'' The simple words said it all. ''Been one all my life. I may be retired, but I'm still a cop. But if you need it spelled out—no, I wouldn't do it.''

Tillie approached them, her arm tucked through Christy's, picking the way through the dirt in her purple tennies. Her brows were drawn together in a slight frown. ''I think those two men up there are getting quite concerned about us. Should we wave to show we're friendly? Even if they are quite rude.''

"Rude?" Jack blinked at her. "What've they done?"

Tillie tossed an indignant glance up the hill. "One of the signs they have says that use of deadly force is authorized."

"I told you that while we were in the car."

"That must be what Walter meant," Tillie muttered, frowning at the sign in question.

Shane stiffened. "Walter? What did he say?"

Grinning, Christy wondered when he would realize he no longer questioned Walter's existence. Whenever it happened, she wanted to be there.

"That's the problem," Tillie fumed. "Walter never really *says* anything. At least not the way we talk. I think he likes to be enigmatic. His messages are not clear at all. Then, of course, if I misunderstand, it's all my fault."

Patient, at least with Tillie, Shane tried again. "What do you *think* he was trying to say?" Hearing his own words, he stopped, his gaze resting on Christy's amused face.

"Trouble," Tillie offered. "Danger. Caution."

Jack lifted his sunglasses to get a better look at her. "And what conclusion did *you* come to?"

Tillie's sigh would have touched the heart of a man harder than Jack. "That he didn't think we should try to get in there." She pointed at the dirt road leading into the restricted area.

"And when did he start sending that particular message?" Jack waited while she thought.

"Just about the time we started talking about it," she decided.

Exhaling noisily, Jack glared at her. "And you didn't think it was worth mentioning? You tell us everything else he says."

"But, Jack, we were having such fun!"

PLAY

RUN
FOR THE
ROSES

and get
THREE FREE GIFTS!
HOW TO PLAY:

1. With a coin, carefully scratch off the silver box at the right. Then check the claim cha
   see what we have for you — **2 FREE BOOKS** and a **FREE GIFT**—**ALL YOURS FR**

2. Send back the card and you'll receive two brand-new Silhouette Romance® novels.
   These books have a cover price of $3.50 each in the U.S. and $3.99 each in Canada,
   they are yours to keep absolutely free.

3. There's no catch. You're under no obligation to buy anything. We charge nothing —
   ZERO — for your first shipment. And you don't have to make any minimum number
   of purchases — not even one!

4. The fact is, thousands of readers enjoy receiving books by mail from the Silhouette
   Reader Service™. They enjoy the convenience of home delivery...they like getting the
   new novels at discount prices, BEFORE they're available in stores... and they love th
   Heart to Heart subscriber newsletter featuring author news, horoscopes, recipes, bo
   reviews and much more!

5. We hope that after receiving your free books you'll want to remain a subscriber. But
   choice is yours — to continue or cancel, any time at all! So why not take us up on
   invitation, with no risk of any kind. You'll be glad you did!

Visit us online at
www.eHarlequin.co

This surprise mystery gift
Could be yours **FREE** –
When you play
RUN for the ROSES

The Silhouette Reader Service™ — Here's how it works:

Chapter Six

"**I** can't believe I let you talk me into this." Christy clutched the reins attached to the bridle on the brown horse and looked down from where she sat in the roomy saddle. It seemed a long way to the ground. It *was* a long way, she reminded herself. If Shane hadn't given her a helping hand, she would have needed a ladder to climb on.

"You're a natural," he assured her, hiding a half grin when she muttered and yanked at the brim of the creamy Stetson he'd insisted she wear. She had coiled her glorious hair up before she'd put it on, and now strands were slipping down, clinging to her temples. Shaded by the brim of the hat, her eyes were a deep green. A mildly annoyed deep green.

Christy sighed. "Yeah, but a natural what? Pushover? Why didn't I just ignore you this morning?"

"Because you couldn't?" He nudged Milt closer to her horse, Belle.

"The fact that I didn't want you disturbing Aunt Tillie might have had something to do with it," she said dryly. "Just how long would you have banged on my bedroom window if I hadn't opened it?"

"I'd still be there."

"That's what I figured." She knew a determined man when she saw one, and that's what had been leaning against the RV, tapping on the window when she pushed aside the curtains. Which was precisely why she had broken a world record in the shower and slid into her light blue jeans and comfortably worn cowboy boots, pulled a raspberry sleeveless shirt over her head, and slipped out the front door in less than ten minutes. "So why the crack of dawn?"

"That's when things start around here. I thought you'd like to see the ranch from a cowman's point of view."

"Which is from the back of a horse?"

He nodded, his voice bland. "That's usually the way. Sometimes we break down and use a pickup or the Jeep. Every now and then we even pull out the helicopter."

Christy looked at him, studying his face to see if he was serious. "You have a helicopter?"

Shane shrugged. "Just a little one. It's a quick way to check the herds."

Just a *little* one? Stunned, she accidentally jiggled the reins and jumped when Belle snorted. Letting out a long breath when the old mare just kept plodding along beside Milt, Christy took another look around her. This time she saw it through new eyes. The rambling old house and the impressive barn were in top-notch condition; they lacked nothing that money and sweat could provide. Apparently, at least judging by the difficulty he'd had in pointing out the ranch's boundaries, the land for miles around belonged to Shane. Add a helicopter to that and what do you have? she asked herself.

A very rich man.

And that meant another black mark on her mental checklist. Now he matched her exes in every respect: an unflagging focus on his work, into control in a big way, hard-edged, worth a bundle and wanted a woman—on his terms. It was not a pretty picture.

Granted, he was devoting time to her. A lot of time. But then, so had numbers one, two and three— at least when they were in hunting mode. She had eventually decided that it was part of their tunnel vision syndrome. Once they'd put a ring on her finger, their attention veered right back to work.

"Let's go this way," Shane said, indicating a worn path. "I want to show you something." Milt ambled down the trail as if he had every step memorized, and Belle obligingly followed. It wasn't long before they stopped in a bower of greenery, presided over by a couple of majestic cottonwood trees.

Shane dismounted in a lithe move that made it look easy, but Christy wasn't fooled. Two hours of riding had already taught her that nothing about it was that simple. She eyed the ground, wondering how she was going to get down, but before she had time to worry, Shane reached up and plucked her from the saddle.

His big, callused hands stayed at her waist until her toes touched the ground—after her body slid down every hard inch of his, pushing her worries about the horse from her mind.

"Okay?"

She nodded and let go of his shirt, expelling a long, shuddering breath. He was driving her crazy and he knew exactly what he was doing. He had a powerful arsenal of sensual moves, and she had a hunch he measured her every shiver and fluttering pulse the way a cat eyed a panicky mouse.

With a great deal of satisfaction.

But she had sworn off men like Shane McBride, she reminded herself grimly. For several very good reasons. So, right now, her number one priority was her career, and her goal was to be sitting behind an editor's desk before her twenty-eighth birthday. Which left her the grand total of nine months.

Okay, so he had a body that made her hormones sit up and howl, as well as a take-charge attitude that could be very appealing—at times. But she still wouldn't fall into bed with him. It didn't matter how good she felt when his fingertips cruised up her spine; she'd just have to ignore the heated sensation, because her bottom line was to leave his ranch with a whole heart in two weeks and two days.

"Come on."

Scattering her thoughts, he took her hand and led her down a narrow path leading through an arch of green tendrils. Even this trail, as far from the house as it was, had been well tended, she realized with surprise.

"This way."

They walked up a few plank steps to a sturdy, low wooden bridge spanning a wide stream. Lacing his fingers through hers, Shane walked to the center and stopped, resting his forearms on the rail. They watched in silence as the clear water tumbled over the rocks below, frothy and sparkling in the dappled sunlight.

"Want to sit here?" Shane walked a few steps over to a large tree with spreading limbs. He patted the waist-high branch next to him. Nodding, Christy swung a leg over the top and settled neatly into place.

Shane wrapped his arm around her waist, securing her. It was a friendly gesture, she realized, protective. His potent masculine awareness was tamped down— at least for the moment. She didn't understand how he turned it off and on, but taking advantage of the mood, she relaxed and draped her arm across his shoulders, leaning against him. Tilting her face to the sun, she brushed the Stetson back, letting it fall to the ground.

Looking around with a sense of familiarity, she said, "This reminds me of something your great-grandmother wrote in her diary. She described a place very much like this, with a stream. She called it her refuge and would sneak away to it when life became too hectic."

"So you're reading it?"

She nodded. "Don't sound so surprised. I told you I would when I borrowed it. It's very touching the way she describes the loneliness, distant neighbors, quilting parties, and how they helped each other in tough times. I'm very impressed by their strength. I would've made a rotten pioneer."

His hand tightened at her waist. "Why do you say that?"

"Because I'm too attached to my bathtub and air-conditioning." She grinned and ruffled his hair.

Pointing to the other bank, where a heavy wooden table and benches nestled against the trees, she said, "I see someone makes use of the place."

"My mother used to come here," Shane said. "She'd pack a lunch, bring a book, read or take a nap."

Used to. Christy's hand tightened on his shoulder, her intuitive recognition of sadness almost stopping her breath, because she knew what was coming. No, she didn't have Aunt Tillie's psychic advantage, she had often explained to her curious cousins, just a sensitivity to moods that was not always comforting.

Right now, she didn't want to hear the words, but she knew he needed to say them, to utter them to someone who would understand that he still had emptiness inside him, that he still ached. "What happened?" she asked, her voice soft.

He let out a long sigh and locked his gaze on the restless water below. "Three years ago she and my dad were returning from a trip. They were tired, anxious to get home, driving too fast. A tire blew, the car flew off the road and hit a tree. They died three miles from home."

The words were brief, but they didn't come easy. He was obviously a man who kept his pain to himself, she thought, impulsively turning to give him a long hug. "I'm sorry," she whispered, tucking her face against his neck, her fingers digging into his shoulders as she thought of her parents. Still slim and youthful, they were retired, living in a condo in La Jolla and dashing off at a moment's notice when the urge to travel hit them. "I can't even imagine how I'd feel if it happened to my parents."

"I hope to God you never find out."

Christy remained where she was, letting her closeness comfort him. After a long moment, he cleared his throat.

"I didn't mean to—"

"Don't." She touched her fingers to his lips, stopping the words. "Let it be." Her heart made a slow cartwheel when she felt the soft touch of his lips in her hair.

Touched, and aware of her own vulnerability to Shane, she dropped her hand to his and gave it a quick squeeze. "Where are we going next?" she asked, breezily. "Do I have to get back on Belle or can I walk?"

"To see some of the best grazing land in the state." Shane gave her a half smile designed to drive women crazy and held her hand as she turned and slid down, landing lightly on her feet. "And you ride."

Damn straight she rode, he thought, watching the tantalizing sway of her bottom as he followed her back. Lifting her on and off the horse was the only chance he had to hold her, and he wasn't about to miss the feel of her soft body against—

A familiar trill split the quiet. Shane pulled the phone from his pocket and gave it a look of sheer disgust. Flipping it open, he snarled, "Hank, I told you—"

"Oh." At the sound of Tillie's breathless voice,

he closed his eyes and heaved a long sigh. "I thought you might be upset because I called, but you're angry at Hank. That's a relief, but what that nice man has done to make you—"

"I am not mad at Hank." Shane spaced his words deliberately.

"Are you sure?" Tillie's chirpy voice sounded doubtful.

"Positive."

"I think perhaps I'd better talk to Hank. Warn him not to call you while you're—"

"*Tillie*. Did you call me for a reason or just to drive me nuts?" Shane scowled at Christy, who was trying her best not to laugh.

"Oh, dear. You *are* angry. Anger is a destructive force, Shane, dear. At least to me. It's like a short circuit."

He took the phone from his ear and seared it with a look. Returning it, he said blankly, "A short circuit?"

"Exactly. I was certain you'd understand. I knew the moment I saw your shirt that—"

"What does my shirt have to do with—" He narrowed his eyes and shot Christy another menacing glance. "Damn it, Tillie, what are we talking about here?"

"Anger." Her voice was patient. "A destructive force that short circuits my..."

"Your *what?*"

"My memory, of course. Oh! I just remembered why I called. Thank you, dear. I knew you'd help. Why only yesterday, Walter told me—"

"Tillie, I pride myself on being a patient man."

Shane ignored Christy's astounded expression. "But I don't want to hear about my shirt, and I don't want to hear about Walter. Just once, will you please stick to whatever is the subject and tell me why you called?"

"About the stars."

Shane drew in a long breath. "What about them?"

"Well, it's really only one. One in particular, that is. The one that falls."

Rubbing his forehead, he tried again. "And what am I supposed to do about it?"

"You? Oh, nothing. Nothing at all. It's Christy. She has to watch it. Tonight, of course."

"Okay," he said with a deep sigh. "I'll tell her."

"I do enjoy our little chats, dear, but you mustn't keep me. Ruth Ann is holding a dowsing lesson."

He blinked when a click followed her last word. "I'm glad I don't have to do business with her. She'd have me so crazy I'd probably sign over the ranch to her."

Christy's laughter rang out in the sudden stillness, startling a bird into flight. She dropped down on a mossy tree stump and swiped at the tears gathered in the corners of her eyes. Watching Shane pocket the phone, she said in a shaky voice, "If you could see your expression. Your face turns a fascinating shade of maroon when you talk with her."

"It's a wonder I don't have a damn stroke. She's enough to—"

"I know." Christy nodded, pulling a tissue from her pocket and dabbing at her eyes. "It just takes a while to get used to her. What did she want?"

"That's a good question." He tugged at her hand

and led her back to the horses. "A great one, in fact. If you sift through Walter, my shirt and Hank, you get stars. And you're supposed to do something about one that falls. That's as close as I can come."

After tossing her back on Belle, he let one hand slide down her thigh, his fingers savoring the warmth of her skin beneath the soft jeans. "Does it make any sense to you?"

She nodded. "Surprisingly enough, it does. Let's go find that grass, and I'll tell you all about it."

"The stars," he prompted a few minutes later as they looked down into a valley covered with the thickest, greenest grass Christy had ever seen. And more cattle than she had ever imagined seeing in one place.

"Lucky cattle," she murmured. "If they just stand still, the grass will simply grow around them."

Patient, he repeated, "The stars."

"I'm a stargazer from way back," she began obediently. "Aunt Tillie knows I'm hooked on the heavens, so to speak."

His dark brows rose. "Do you have a telescope?"

"Had. A small one at home in San Diego." She sighed. "For all the good it did me. The city lights dim the stars, and I couldn't see enough to make it worthwhile."

"And what's special about tonight?"

Christy smiled. "I imagine Uncle Walter told Aunt Tillie some hot news about a falling star. She probably thought I'd enjoy watching it. And I will. At least I brought along my binoculars."

Shane smiled and reached for her hand. Lifting it to his mouth, he brushed his lips across her knuckles, enjoying the flustered look in her eyes. "Lady, you're in luck. I just happen to have one of the best telescopes on the market set up on my deck."

Christy rapped on the kitchen door, pulled it open and stuck her head in. "Hi, Adelaide."

"Girl, how many times have I told you to just walk in? Every time you knock, I have to come runnin' and I'm too old for that nonsense. Oh, I know. You were raised proper, and you don't think it's right to go traipsin' through someone's house, but I'm tellin' you that you're wearin' out my knee bones."

Christy grinned at Shane's tall, angular housekeeper. Gray hair dyed a flaming red, her usual uniform was worn jeans, equally worn sweatshirt and bright tennies that made Tillie's mouth water. She proudly boasted she had a collection of them that made Imelda Marcos look like a pauper.

The self-appointed McBride family historian, she described herself as Shane's kissin' cousin. Shane, she explained with a rich laugh, didn't know if it was true or not. He couldn't follow the convoluted family lines of second and third cousins. Didn't much care, either.

Watching Adelaide pounce on a water spot with a paper towel, Christy recalled Shane's description of meeting his housekeeper. The day before his parents' funeral, she had pounded on the front door, opened it, dropped her large suitcase inside and introduced herself. Grabbing his arm, she had dragged him through the house, announced she would take the bedroom and bath off the kitchen and named her salary. Not waiting for a response, she unpacked and began cleaning the kitchen cupboards.

She ran a tight ship, Shane had said with a grin. She couldn't cook worth a damn, but she kept everyone hopping and refused his periodic offers to raise her salary. She just shooed him away and said she'd tell him when she wanted more money.

Within moments of meeting Adelaide, Christy had recognized the older woman's true value. She provided some of the warmth and sense of family Shane had lost three years earlier. Anyone could clean his house, but this woman helped fill the emptiness in his heart.

"I'm a little early," Christy said, interrupting Adelaide's flow of words. Talking to the housekeeper, she had learned, was like talking to Tillie. You had to be ruthless; it didn't do any good to wait for the one-sided conversation to die.

The older woman gave her a sharp look, taking in her creamy slacks and the matching sweater draped over her shoulders, complementing the rose-colored knit shirt beneath. "Somehow I don't think Shane will mind havin' a pretty woman waitin' for him. Well," exasperation sharpened her voice, "are you gonna find him, or do I have to go out and tell him you're here, then run back in and tell you to go on out?"

"No, I'll go."

Christy grinned but made a mental note to be cautious around the housekeeper. There was a gleam in her hazel eyes that was all too familiar. She had a nasty hunch that Adelaide and Tillie were charter members of the same matchmakers club.

Stepping toward the deck outside the dining area, Christy stopped when Adelaide said, "Not that way." She pointed behind her. "Go down the hall, in Shane's bedroom."

Narrowing her eyes, Christy said evenly, "Perhaps you should let him know I'm here."

Adelaide shook her head and heaved a gusty sigh. "It's just a bedroom, girl. Not Sin City. And I'm not the madam of a brothel. Walk through the room and out the sliding glass door to the deck. He's got his paraphernalia out there."

Christy turned, feeling the heat in her face, and followed the housekeeper's pointing finger. She was getting paranoid, she admitted silently, as she walked through the living room. But that seemed to come with the territory of having a matchmaking aunt. Any one of Tillie's nieces or nephews would understand perfectly.

Stopping to run her fingers down the rough stone of the fireplace, Christy admired the large, high-ceilinged room. Several rugs dotted the gleaming oak floors, large, comfortable-looking chairs and sofas were placed around the hearth while hand-rubbed bookcases and chests held pride of place along the walls between large windows. It was a blend of comfort and elegance that she found charming.

She walked down the lighted hallway, stopping to admire family photos. The latest caught Shane laughing with an older couple, obviously his parents. Looking at his father, a big man with black eyes and brows topped by salt-and-pepper hair, Christy knew exactly what Shane would look like in another thirty years—impressive and very sexy.

Following the lights, she stepped into Shane's bedroom, where a bed the size of Rhode Island held her fascinated gaze. The room itself, she eventually noted, was a blend of browns and blues, masculine and attractive. A brighter light on the deck lured her outside. Stepping through the open sliding glass door, she called, "Shane?"

"Up here."

His deep voice ruffled her nerve endings, and she stopped a moment, taking a deep breath. For a woman who had sworn off men, she was pathetic, Christy told herself in disgust. Why couldn't she simply walk up the spiral staircase jutting from the deck to the roof and join him on the sturdy platform as she would anyone else?

The answer wasn't long in coming: because he wasn't anyone else. It was that simple and that terrifying. Shane was more than a man with a muscular body, cleft chin and black eyes. He was caring, and sexy, a man made wary by the wrong women. And sexy.

And he appealed to her at a level that had never been touched by a man.

Silently, she sorted through her priorities again— freedom, an editorial position, Los Angeles. Men were not on the list. Not even one like Shane, who quite literally took away her breath.

"Christy?" Mild impatience laced his voice.

"Yes?"

"Are you all right?"

"Oh yeah, just dandy."

"Well, then, come up here."

She stepped on the first tread, thinking, *come into my parlor...*

Chapter Seven

"You look good enough to eat."

At the sound of his deep voice, Christy stopped at the last turn of the stairway. Looking up at him, she had one thought: if she was smart, she'd turn around and hightail it back to the RV. Shane looked like a big cat ready to pounce. He sounded the same way: edgy, expectant and very sure of himself.

His hair still damp from a shower, he wore another denim shirt with the familiar swirl of stars on the pocket tucked in his jeans, and highly polished boots. And, damn it all, he looked too good to walk—or run—away from.

"You must buy those shirts by the gross," she blurted.

He gave her one of his killer half smiles. "Close. A couple dozen at a time. They're cut larger in the shoulders, so they're comfortable. Dull, huh?"

Christy swallowed. Dull was not the word for the

big dark-haired, dark-eyed man looking down at her. *Dull* didn't even belong in the same county with him. Reminding herself that she was a woman with a mission, a long-term plan that didn't include him or any other man, she ascended the last few stairs.

Taking her hand when she reached the top, Shane kept her beside him, giving her an opportunity to look around. The platform was larger than she had expected, holding a patio table and chairs, the large telescope and a wide chaise longue in an upright position. Concealed from the front of the house, the platform was level with the peak of the roof and had an unrestricted view of the sky.

Drawing her closer, Shane slowly dipped his head, giving her time to protest. When she didn't, he nuzzled her hair, inhaling the fragrance of her shampoo, then covered her mouth in a lingering kiss. "Nice," he murmured. "Strawberries."

"Don't push me, McBride." She gave him an aggravated look, hoping he couldn't feel her heart tripping in double time.

Swinging her around before she could do more than blink, he gestured toward the edge of the platform. "Are you comfortable with heights?"

She tugged her hand from his and, stepping around him, ran her fingers along the waist-high railing. "I'm fine as long as there's something between me and the ground."

"Then hold on to the rail and stay there while I switch off all the lights." Narrowing his eyes, he hesitated then shook his head. "No, bad plan. Come with me." He held out his hand.

"Why?" Her brows rose at the command. "I'm

fine here." He wasn't going to move without her, she realized after several seconds passed. He would stand there, waiting for the rest of the night if that's what it took. Stalling long enough to annoy him, she finally exhaled noisily and took his hand, moving with him to the light switch no more than six feet away.

"I don't know why I needed a chaperon to walk a few—" Her breath caught when he hit the button, simultaneously turning off the lights on the platform, the stairs, the deck below and his bedroom, throwing them into the total darkness of a new moon. In the clarity of the desert air, the glittering stars poised in the ebony sky looked close enough to touch.

"Oh, Shane, *look* at them," she finally managed to say. Remaining where she was until her eyes adjusted to the enveloping darkness, she felt like a kid in a candy store: awash with longing, wanting to reach out and grab her favorites.

Even as a child, she'd had a love affair with the star-studded darkness above. When weather permitted, she'd begged to sleep outside, not caring if she ended up in the backyard or the flatbed of a pickup truck. Her parents, both amateur astronomers, pleased themselves by indulging her.

At first, these ventures took place in full moonlight when she could see only the brighter stars and planets and not be confused by myriads of fainter stars. In that way, she learned the names of constellations and the related myths of the Greeks and Romans at the same time she practiced her *ABC*s. Later, in the darker nights of the new moon, she observed fainter stars, nebulae, planets and minor constellations.

Now, Christy took in the magnificence above her as greedily as the desert absorbed moisture during summer storms. "Oh, look," she said as she pointed, "there's Orion's sword. I've never seen it this clearly. And over there, next to Boötes," she added, pointing to a semicircular arc, "the Corona Borealis."

Standing behind Christy, Shane slid his arms around her waist, holding her against him as she looked straight up, pleased and amused by her excitement. "Are you cold? You shivered."

She shook her head absently, the movement fanning her hair across his chest. "Just excited."

Shane's body tightened. He had felt that same shiver, when he'd touched her, kissed her. Now it had a name: excitement. The quick shudder was more than that, though. It was an ageless response to a man's proximity to a woman, to mutual attraction—and it was sexy as hell. He couldn't wait to feel it when he had her in his bed, naked and climbing all over him.

Forcing a lightness he didn't feel, he gave her a squeeze. "Poor, little city girl. You've never really seen the sky before."

"Only a few times like this," she admitted. "Once at Crater Lake in Oregon. It was so incredible, I don't think I slept until dawn." It had been more than twenty years earlier on a dark night with a brilliant star-studded sky, and she had been a child who had believed all things were possible. And with a seven-year-old girl's determination, she had resolved to discover a star, to have her very own place in the universe. The dream had never faded, nor had the determination, and it was still a secret held close to her heart. Perhaps it was simply ego, but one day a star would be hers.

"It's very rare to find a place like this," she murmured, taking pleasure in his warmth at her back. "Somewhere with an almost total absence of man-made light. Cities, with all their streetlights and neon signs, have all but obliterated the stars."

"Since you've been here, you must have stayed outside to look at them after I've taken you home." It was a statement, not a question.

"I have, but several of the seniors are night owls and there were always lights on. It didn't come close to this." Lifting a hand toward the distant stars, she said, "This is…breathtaking."

Yeah, that was the word, all right, he thought, looking down at her. Breathtaking. Exciting. And sexy beyond belief.

Easing back, he deliberately put a few inches of space between them. He wanted to keep her right where she was, in his arms, pressing back against him, but in another few seconds his body would take over and she'd know exactly what he was thinking and feeling. He doubted if she'd stick around long after that.

He cleared his throat. "Do you want to use the telescope now?"

"Not yet." She shook her head, still gazing upward. "Right now, I want to see the whole sky. Take in as much as I can." But casting a quick glance at the scope and its impressive apparatus, she realized he had been right earlier. He did indeed have the best money could buy.

With a sudden grin, she said, "You should invite Aunt Tillie up here to use the telescope. She'd be thrilled."

He looked at her in surprise. "I didn't know she's interested in stars."

Christy's grin grew wider. "She isn't. Not a bit. But with that thing, she could probably find some of those little gray men flying around. Just think what a hit you'd be with her. Who knows? She'd probably do something very special for you."

"Like what?" He knew he hadn't kept the apprehension out of his voice when she chuckled.

"Umm, maybe like take you with her when she visits another planet."

With a shout of laughter, Shane scooped her up, whirling her around in a circle. Startled, Christy clasped her hands behind his neck and hung on. When he sat on the chaise, he kept her close, lifting her so she sat across his legs, half facing him, her arms still draped loosely around his shoulders. Ignoring the demands of his hardening body, he decided to keep her right where she was, leaning contentedly against him.

The corner of his mouth curved up. "I don't even want to think about it. Hell, right now she only likes me a little, and she drives me nuts. She calls me with the craziest excuses every time—"

He stopped as if he had run into a solid steel wall, remembering with great clarity exactly when she had called. Tillie had used her spooky phone system each time he'd had her niece in his arms, thinking that he wanted to drag her to his bed.

"Every time what?"

"Damn it, can she see us?" he demanded abruptly. "When we're together? Like this?"

Christy laughed, delighted with his appalled expression. "I wondered when that would occur to you."

"*Can* she?" His arms tightened around her waist.

"I...don't know." She tilted her head, thinking. "I've wondered that myself. If you remember, I mentioned the other night that she has an incredible sense of timing." He looked so stunned, she couldn't resist twisting the knife a bit. "Come to think of it, she has gotten me out of a couple of dicey situations in the past."

"Well, hell."

"She's always been very protective of her nieces," she murmured, lacing her fingers in his hair. "But then, there have been a number of times when she *hasn't* called."

His brows rose. "Really?"

"Yep."

"Then I think..." Looking into her eyes, he forgot what he thought. He only knew what he wanted, needed. Sliding one hand into her silky hair, he eased her closer, slowly, giving her another chance to protest. When she murmured a small sound of approval instead, he fit his mouth to hers.

The kiss was meant to be a tender exploration, but dizzy from the touch of her tongue against his and her beaded nipples pressing into his chest, he tightened his arms and leaned back in the chaise, taking her with him. One of his large hands shifted to her bottom, holding her closer, shifting her until she covered his aching body.

Primitive instincts took over, until his entire focus narrowed to Christy—her pliant body moving restlessly against his, her feminine yet defiant fragrance, the soft sensual sounds deep in her throat. Blood pounded through his veins, and he knew he wouldn't stop this time until—

The trill of his cellular phone had the effect of someone dousing him with ice water. Tightening his hands on Christy's shoulders, he lifted her off his chest and gave her a look of pure frustration. "If your aunt *can* see us," he said between clenched teeth, "she doesn't have the survival instincts of a slug."

Dazed, Christy nodded. Her heart still raced and she didn't have the slightest idea what he was talking about.

Shane moved her beside him and tucked his arm around her shoulders before he slammed his hand on the glass-topped table next to the chaise, almost crushing the phone. He inhaled and let the air out in a slow steady stream before he raised it to his ear. "Yes, Tillie."

"Shane," she chirped, "did you see it?"

"It?" He closed his eyes, trying to clear his head.

"*It,*" she emphasized. "The star. The one that fell."

"Well—"

"Something like that doesn't happen often."

"You're right." Thinking of the way Christy's lips had clung to his, he shuddered.

"I'm sure it made quite an impression on Christy."

"I'm counting on it."

"Ah, to be young and experience the full joy of these events again." Tillie's sigh was the tiniest bit envious.

Shane's eyes flew open. "I beg your pardon?"

"To see the stars clearly, without glasses. Especially bifocals," she said darkly. "It simply doesn't matter what you do, that dratted line is always blurring things. But then, I don't suppose you know about that. I'm sure your vision is perfect."

"Yeah, perfect." He met Christy's wary gaze as she sat up and straightened her shirt. Of course his hindsight was even better.

"We turned off all the lights," Tillie said, "then laid on blankets, so our necks wouldn't get stiff. It worked just fine, except that the ground was still a bit damp and we got chilled. Did you?"

"No, we weren't cold." He heard voices raised in the background and Tillie agreeing with something.

"I almost forgot why I called," she said hastily. "Ben made some brownies and homemade ice cream. He said if you can tear yourselves away, come join us." Her voice perplexed, she added, "He laughed when he said it, but I'm sure he meant it."

"Thanks, Tillie. We'll be there."

Shane replaced the phone and looked up at Christy. She was busily—and unnecessarily—brushing off her slacks. "We've been invited for dessert," he said briefly.

"You want to go?" Her gaze met his for a moment before it darted away.

"Hell, no." He frowned, not believing she could even ask. "But I figure you'd prefer that to ripping each other's clothes off and—"

"Let's go." Christy turned and took a step toward the stairs, coming to a dead stop when Shane's hand locked around her arm.

"Honey, I'm sorry." His fingers relaxed but he didn't release her. "I didn't plan this. The invitation was to look at stars, and that's all I meant to do."

"I know." She believed him. He wasn't the type to lure a woman—her—into his arms and bed with lies. He was too direct, too honest. Too honorable. He didn't bother to hide the fact that he wanted her; in fact, he was very clear about that—every time they met. And the truth was, Shane McBride didn't have to lie. He could make any woman weak in the knees just by looking at her with his bright, hungry eyes.

Clearing her throat, she said again, "I know you didn't plan it." And that was the terrifying part. That they could reach flash point while laughing over something silly. "Are you ready to leave?"

He nodded. "Let me get the lights."

On the way downstairs, determined to lighten the mood, she said, "I love vanilla with chocolate syrup. How do you like your ice cream?"

"Right now? On my lap."

"You'll send it out right away? A week? Thanks. Nice doing business with you." Shane hung up the phone on his desk and slid his credit card back in his wallet. He hadn't been sure he'd be able to locate the exact item, but he'd done it, and in plenty of time. Pleased with the transaction, he leaned back in the swivel chair. It was the perfect gift, he reflected. Unless he was way off base, Christy would like it.

Grinning at the understatement, he admitted that what he really wanted was for her to be thrilled right down to her pink-tipped toes.

"Hey, boss." Hank stepped through the doorway.

Shane straightened, alerted by the uneasy expression on the older man's face. Hank had been the ranch foreman since before he was born, going back to the days his dad and Hank were best friends. Calling Shane *boss* was more a title of respect and affection than the truth, and it wasn't often he came to the office in need of advice. "What's up?"

"Nothin' about the work," Hank said, easing down in the chair across from Shane and stretching out his long legs. "It's that little, curly-headed woman."

Shane's brows rose. "Tillie."

"Yep."

Grinning, Shane thought back over the past few days. He had expected the seniors to take off every day, looking for ways to infiltrate Area 51—and from what he'd gathered of their conversations, that had been their original plan. But their one trip out there, combined with the idiot Starman's prediction at lunch and multiple messages Walter sent via intercelestial airwaves had convinced them that nighttime was the witching hour, and the arena was to be the sky above.

Accordingly, they had devised a duty roster: four seniors per five-hour shifts, running from eight at night to six in the morning. They sat in the clearing beyond the RVs in lawn chairs, facing one another so they could visit, each responsible for observing the quadrant of sky they faced.

Their nocturnal duties had drastically cut down their daytime activities, leaving them with few choices beyond joining Ruth Ann's dowsing crew or pestering the hands.

"What's she doing? Interfering with the men?"

"Nope." Hank answered the last question first. "To tell the truth, the men are gettin' a kick out of the whole bunch. Skip's as happy as a jaybird guttin' that old Ford pickup and puttin' it back together. Opal, his wife, has the men goggle-eyed with all her palm readin', and Melinda's talkin' to a few who are interested about investin' their money. You know what gets me?"

Shane shook his head.

"They're all real smart and every last one of them thinks they're gonna see a UFO."

"Yeah, that's why they're here. So what's the problem?"

"The little one with the weird clothes. Tillie."

Shane cleared his throat, determined not to laugh. Hank was serious, and baffled. "What? You guys can't handle a woman no bigger than a kid? What's she doing?"

"It ain't so much what she's doin', it's what she *wants* to do."

Checking his watch, Shane said, "Let's move along here, Hank. Neither of us wants to miss dinner." The thought of Ben's meals had his gaze switching to the calendar. Nine more meals. Nine more days before they left. Nine more days before Christy—

"She wants to play poker with the men. In the

bunkhouse.'' Hank shot him a worried look. ''Is that okay?''

Shane shrugged. ''How do the men feel about it? It's their bunkhouse.''

''Hell.'' Hank made a noise that sounded like a snort. ''They think it's funny. They're lookin' forward to it.''

''Then what's the problem?''

Hank reddened. ''They're the problem. They cuss—hell, we all cuss—somethin' awful, and she's such a sweet little thing. They drink, too.''

''I imagine she's seen her share of both. She's no spring chicken, you know.'' But he understood the problem. Hank was a throwback to earlier days when men didn't swear, drink or play cards around women. A bachelor all his life, he had an old-fashioned sense of chivalry that was rare in this day and age. And he was so shy around women, he was all but tongue-tied.

''I wouldn't worry about it,'' he told Hank. ''I think they'll be okay. There's something about Tillie that brings out the best in people.'' Looking at his watch again, he said, ''Let's go eat.''

Dinner was a noisy affair. The seniors had continued setting tables outside in the shade, and soon the hands had brought out similar tables. At first, the men had remained apart, eating silently while listening to the seniors speculate about UFOs and aliens. It hadn't taken long before the hands began telling stories of lights in the sky and other aberrations they'd witnessed to the fascinated, captivated audience.

At one time or another, all of the men had seen

something. Most of them were born and raised in the area and took the sightings with several grains of salt. Patriotic to the marrow, it was enough for them that the government owned the property. If the Air Force wanted to experiment with aircraft, it was fine with them. Not one of the pragmatic men had ever considered the possibility of aliens roaming the skies. But the visitors were the best audience they'd ever had, and if *they* wanted to believe in aliens, that was just fine. No one else had ever taken notes while they'd talked; in fact, most people around there were just tired of all the fuss.

So the stories flowed and the listeners asked questions and jotted in spiral-bound books. Tillie, enchanted with each tale, just egged them on with her wide-eyed expression of delight.

Shane sat next to Christy, watching amusement brighten her face as she listened to Red spin a tale about tracking a bright star that turned out to be an airplane dropping drugs. As usual, he battled the tension that gripped his body whenever he was close to her. Whenever he thought of her. Hell, when he got up in the morning, knowing she was within fifty miles of him.

Her wariness these past two days and the memories of their explosive encounter on the platform were slowly driving him mad. Since then, she'd made sure they weren't alone.

His campaign wasn't working, he brooded, listening to her peal of laughter when Red hit the punch line. What had begun as a simple plan—snagging a cook, inviting the group for a three-week stay and having Christy in his arms and bed for the duration—was not working. In this case, two out of three was a pathetic score. But he still had nine days, he thought, his eyes narrowed in determination. A lot could happen in nine days.

Later that evening, after realizing she'd disappeared for the third night in a row, he knocked on the door of Christy's RV.

"Come in."

Shane pushed open the door and scowled at her. "What are you doing holed up in here?"

Making a shooing motion with her hand, Christy kept her gaze on the computer screen. "Go away. My second article is due in two days, and I can't make it work."

"That's because your brain cells need air. Let's go for a ride. I can have Milt and Belle ready in two minutes."

Christy gave him an aggravated look. "Are you listening? I've got a deadline. If I don't keep my butt in this chair, I won't make it. If I don't make it, I don't get paid. Worse, yet, I annoy an editor. I don't want to do that." Her frown deepened as she recalled similar conversations with three other men. Shaking her head, she said, "Go away. I'm not stopping until this is ready to go."

"Okay. Fine." Damned if he was going to beg.

"Goodbye."

"Guess I can always sit in on the poker game."

"Fine. Do tha—" Christy looked up and for the first time that evening her green gaze met his straight on, focusing her complete attention on him. "A poker game?"

"Yeah, want to play?" The men would raise

merry hell if he brought another woman in, but he was getting desperate.

"Poker?" Christy hit the save button and jumped to her feet. "Where?"

"At the bunkhouse." Blinking at her sudden enthusiasm, he held open the door.

"Does Aunt Tillie know about it?"

"Know?" He grinned. "She's the one who suggested it."

"Damn! I should have known it would happen. It's the last thing my cousin Brandy told me." She grabbed a light jacket and flipped on the exterior lights.

"What was?"

"That mixing Aunt Tillie with cowboys and poker was a sure recipe for trouble. Let's go."

When she headed for the house, Shane draped his arm over her shoulders and turned her in the opposite direction. "It's at the bunkhouse."

In her rush to get Tillie out of the game before the hands became a lynch mob, she paid little attention to the two-story structure. The main floor, she noted absently when Shane ushered her inside, seemed to be community property, with a kitchen, utility room and a huge catchall room holding a pool table, computer, TV, sofas and chairs along with a large, round card table. Presumably individual rooms were upstairs.

Tillie sat at the table surrounded by four rugged men. She wore her favorite outfit of green lace held together with an orange elastic belt. The ensemble was completed with a green visor, shading her forehead, and a mountainous stack of toothpicks in front of her. The men wore baffled expressions.

"Aunt Tillie," Christy began in a soothing tone, planning to yank her errant aunt out of the game.

"Ah, Christy." Her aunt's blue eyes shone with joy. "Hank, Red, Murray and Nick are showing me some of the finer points of the game. We're playing..." She looked at the men for help.

"Seven card stud," they chorused.

"Looks like they're pretty good teachers." Shane looked pointedly at the skimpy clumps of toothpicks before each man.

"We got thrown off our rhythm a bit," Red admitted. "Miss Tillie has a habit of tossing cards aside if she don't think we should have them."

"Well, I can't think of any reason you'd want a ten if it ruins a perfectly good straight," she protested, still not convinced they were right. "If you'd just be patient, the right card would come along."

"Just deal 'em, Tillie," Nick said, squinting through his bifocals. "All of 'em. And call 'em the way we showed you."

Tillie shuffled the cards with a flourish and began dealing. "Two cards down, right?"

"Right." They all nodded, watching her with narrowed eyes.

"Aunt Tillie, I really think we should—"

"Not now, dear. I have to concentrate. Jack," she murmured. "Ten, five, a queen, and dealer has an ace. Ace is high." She looked up. "Is that right? I bet?"

They nodded. She shoved in three toothpicks, waited for them and dealt the next round. "Three,

three—I mean treys, six, two and a four. Dealer is still high.'' Three more toothpicks went into the pot, each of the men following suit.

"King, eight, six, a *pair* of sixes there, ten and a queen. Pair of six bets.'' Watching with an eagle eye until all the toothpicks were in, she dealt the cards up again. "Six, seven, four—oh, Nick has a possible straight there—seven, and dealer gets an eight. Pair of sixes is still high.''

"Last card is down,'' Hank reminded her.

Tillie nodded, following instructions. "Two, three, nine, nine and a deuce,'' she said, her brow furrowed with concentration. "Well, that certainly messed up Nick's straight. I think the pair is still high.''

Christy closed her eyes and sighed. She felt Shane jerk and his hand close convulsively on her shoulder. She glanced up at him, lifting her brows in an I-told-you-so look.

Nick broke the charged silence, his voice unsteady. "Yes, ma'am, I'm still high.'' He tossed in several toothpicks, waited for the pot to sweeten, then pushed his pair forward. In silence, the others tossed their cards aside and watched him pull in the pot.

"I think we need a change,'' Hank drawled. "Five card draw. And we'll let Miss Tillie deal.''

The others nodded, never taking their eyes off the petite woman with the silver curls.

Thrilled, Tillie gathered in the cards and shuffled. "I don't know how to thank you. I've learned so much tonight. Usually people don't want to play with me, although I can't understand why.''

"They're all down this time," Hank reminded her, pointing to the deck.

Nodding, she began sliding the cards across the table, facedown. "King, queen, ace, trey and a queen."

Hank's big hand closed over both of hers. "Miss Tillie, tell me something. Do you know what all these cards are? Without looking?"

She nodded, her eyes bright with success. "Oh, yes. I used to have trouble with some of them, but now I get them all right."

Hank looked at the other men, a peculiar expression on his face. They were grinning like lunatics. Giving them a disgusted glance, he turned back to her. "Have you ever thought that some people might get a tad upset when you do that in a game?"

"Why?" When he struggled for an answer, she shook her head. "No, you must be wrong, Hank. When I took all those tests at UCLA—you know, the university in Los Angeles?—they were very excited when I did it."

Red broke the silence with a shout of laughter. "Tillie, how about a game of pool?"

Chapter Eight

"Come on now, admit it. You're having fun."

Christy looked away from the bawling cattle to meet Shane's satisfied gaze. She'd been astride Belle for the past four hours, helping Shane and Red move a small herd to a new grazing area. She had no doubt that they could have handled the job without her, but she was pleased to be along.

"I'm having fun," she said obediently. "Especially now that Belle has quit giving me those nervous looks over her shoulder."

"Yeah, horses are funny that way. Once their riders calm down, they do, too."

He was right, darn it. After just a few days, she had begun to enjoy the daily outings. She certainly wasn't rodeo material, and she still needed help getting on and off, but she had learned to relax and move with the horse instead of against it.

She also liked spending time with Shane, especially when she managed to include at least one other person in the outing. Intelligent, with a wry wit, he was a good companion—if you didn't count the sexual tension that leaped and sizzled between them at the most unexpected times.

Cresting the hill, they looked down on the grazing cattle, watching them spread out in their new pasture.

"What's that?" Christy asked, pointing to a small cloud of pink and purple against the background of emerald-green grass.

Shane shrugged. "Wildflowers, I suppose."

"Can we go look?"

"Sure." He pressed his heels in Milt's sides and they ambled down the hill. "They probably won't look as good up close."

"I'm not after a bouquet, I just want to see what they are."

Something in her tone brought Shane's head around. Her words prompted the memory of Tillie's early morning call, waking him from a sound sleep, and a chill prickled at his nape.

"Shane, dear," she'd chirped, sounding as if she were in a tunnel, "I was wondering—"

He had looked at the illuminated number on the clock and groaned. "Tillie, do you have any idea what time it is?"

"I suppose it's early," she said after a long pause. "I'm standing on my head right now, so I can't see the clock."

"Standing on your—?"

"At any rate, it's too dark to see it, so I suppose it must be *very* early."

He took a deep breath and tried again. "Yeah,

kind of. Why on earth are you standing on your head?''

"Why shouldn't I?" she asked in a reasonable tone. "It's the way I start every morning. It rushes blood to your brain, you know. Of course, this morning I *am* a bit earlier than usual but—''

"Tillie, why are you calling me?''

"That's what I'm telling you. Walter woke me, chatting about flowers.''

Shane froze at the sound of Walter's name, missing the rest of her comment. "Hmm? What did you say.''

Patient with him, she began again. "Walter said something about flowers. It was all very confusing.'' She thought a moment then added, "Flowers always cheer me up, but Walter wasn't happy. Not a bit. So if you are thinking of getting a bouquet for Christy, I'd wait a bit, dear.''

"I wasn't—''

"I'm not at all sure what he meant, but he said something about the flowers being colorful, and pretty is as pretty does.''

Closing his eyes in resignation, Shane wondered just what the hell *that* meant.

"I don't know, either,'' Tillie confessed. "You know Walter, he does like being mysterious.''

Now, looking back over his shoulder at Christy, Shane said, "Tillie called me in the middle of the night.''

"Oh?'' she murmured absently.

"Yeah, Walter made a long distance call to warn me about some flowers.''

She groaned and kept her gaze on the colorful

plants ahead. "I really don't want to hear this. Let's hope she's wrong."

Studying the spreading cluster of plants a few minutes later, she said in a grim voice, "Well, she was right. As usual. You've got a big problem here, Shane. I'm no expert but I'd bet my next paycheck that this is a noxious weed that's giving the Bureau of Land Management fits. It's called Russian knapweed. I ran across a patch of it a year or so ago and believe me, it's nothing but trouble."

"How bad?"

"About as bad as it gets." She leaned over, brushing aside the pink and purple flowers to touch the small, blue-green leaves. "I have no idea what it does to cattle, but I know it can kill horses over a period of several months. Not too long ago, I read that New Mexico has a bad problem with it, especially in the northwest corner along the San Juan river. It's growing everywhere, taking over the land and replacing the native plants and grasses."

Breaking off a small branch, she held it up for him to see. "It's perennial, which means that cutting or pulling won't kill it. As far as I know, chemicals are the best way to get rid of it."

"What kind?" he asked, his voice curt.

She shook her head. "I don't know. I'm strictly an amateur at this. Your best bet is to call the BLM and ask for a weed specialist to pay you a visit. Soon. Like yesterday." Looking up at him, she added, "Are there any other patches of it around?"

Shane shrugged. "I don't know. We've been alerted to the problems with yellow star thistle, so we watch for it, but we haven't heard about any trouble around here with knapweed." He gave a shrill whistle and caught Red's attention. Waving him over, he explained the problem and told him to move the cattle to the far end of the pasture.

Next, he pulled out his phone, poked a series of numbers and spoke to someone at the BLM, arranging for a specialist to come to the ranch the next day. Pocketing the phone, he looked at Christy. "How do you feel about helicopters?"

"I've been on first-name terms with several of them." Turning Belle toward the house, she said, "Let's go."

In less than an hour, they were in the air. Christy rode shotgun, armed with binoculars and a map of the ranch on her lap.

"Over there. About two o'clock." She pointed and Shane angled the copter around for a better look. "That's it, all right," she said. "Now if I can just figure out where we are, I'll mark—" Shane slid his finger to a spot on the map, and she drew a small circle. "Thanks."

For the first time Shane could recall, UFOs were replaced as the main topic of conversation at dinner. Knapweed held center stage.

"Did you cover the whole ranch?" Hank asked.

Shane shook his head. "Only this side of the road."

The men nodded, understanding he meant the grazing land. That was the number one priority.

"We'll leave early in the morning to check the other side, so we'll be back when the BLM guy gets here."

"Boss?" Red slid several sheets of papers down the table to Shane. "I pulled this off the computer when I got back. Wish it said something different, but there's no good news about this stuff at all."

His expression grim, Shane scanned the material then folded the paper and tucked it in his pocket. Meeting Christy's worried gaze, he smiled and lifted his wineglass in a silent toast. "There is an upside," he said, turning to Red. "We were lucky enough to have Christy identify it and we learned today that it's not widespread. It could be a whole lot worse."

"Eeeeeehaw!" Red jumped up and grabbed Christy's hand, pulling her into an impromptu two-step between the tables. Flushed and laughing on the return trip, she gasped when Shane reached out and snagged her, pulling her into his lap.

"Gotcha," he whispered, his breath warm on her ear.

"Ah...I should probably help clear up." She attempted to rise but sank back willingly when his arm tightened around her waist.

"You've already put in a long day," he reminded her, enjoying the way her soft white skirt flared across his jeans. "Relax, I'm not going to bite." Several seconds passed before he murmured, "Yet."

Christy felt her heart leap. Would he always make her pulse pound like this? she wondered, sliding her hand over his larger one at her side. Would the sight of him always kick her hormones into a state of prowling torment? Probably, she decided, leaning back against him, her lips curved up in a private little smile. And she wouldn't have it any other way.

She remained there, perched on his thighs, leaning

against his hard chest, until the soft, insistent voice of reality broke through her contentment. There was no *always* with Shane, it reminded her. Nothing with him—neither her attraction to him nor his reaction to her—was permanent. He'd been very clear about that, giving them three weeks at the most.

And almost two of them were gone.

Her definition of a relationship, the voice prompted, began with love and ended with marriage and a family. His, with a time limitation, was a far cry from hers.

Shane was a man of great tenderness and even greater sensuality, she reflected, as his hand slid down her thigh, fingering the buttons on her skirt. He needed and deserved love more than any man she knew, but he had deliberately cut himself off to that emotion. He opted for sex rather than love and, unfortunately for them both, she was incapable of giving one without the other.

"Do you want to try the telescope tonight?" he asked, his voice a deep rumble. When she turned to him with narrowed eyes, he grinned, holding up his hands in surrender. "No monkey business—just stargazing."

Christy shook her head, telling herself the pang she felt wasn't regret. "I'll have to pass. I have an appointment with a blanket and pillow on the ground, surrounded by seniors. There's supposed to be a meteor shower visible tonight."

"I'll share your blanket," he said promptly. "As soon as it's dark."

Two hours later, Shane spread a blanket on the thick grass next to Skip and Opal and dropped onto it with a sigh. Stretched out on his back, he took up more than his fair share of space. Christy tossed him a pillow and sat beside him. Tillie, Jack, Melinda and Dave sat in the chairs talking softly and scanning their sector of the sky. Ruth Ann and Ben shared a blanket nearby, while Claude and Jim each opted for a chaise longue.

"With each passing day, I'm more convinced that your friend, Starman, is as nutty as a fruitcake," Jack told Tillie, his voice carrying clearly in the crisp, dry air.

Melinda shook her head. "I don't know. Crazy as it seems, I think he believed every word he said. Of course, that doesn't make it true."

"I wonder if he's still eyeballing his spooky friends while they listen in on private phone conversations," Dave commented.

"I still don't see the point." Melinda nudged Jack's leg with her bare toes. "Assuming it's true, what could they learn? A lot of slang? Local gossip? Why would they care what people say?"

Nabbing her ankle, Jack placed her foot on his knee, grinning at her. "Hell, I don't know."

"I told you," Skip called out. "It's to learn how we talk, so they can disguise themselves and pass among us."

"Yeah, right," Jack snorted. "As if no one would notice that they're gray, three feet tall and have huge eyes."

Christy sat tailor fashion on the blanket, smiling at the amiable squabbling. Shifting to a more comfortable spot, she stilled when she met Shane's dark gaze.

"What are you thinking about?" he asked, his voice soft.

She shook her head. "You wouldn't believe it."

"Try me." Patting his shoulder in invitation, he said, "Come down here and tell me about it."

Scooting down beside him and resting her head on his shoulder, she sighed. "This is nice." Actually, she reflected, it was pretty close to terrific. Next to Shane's strong body, she felt... What? Safe? No, she rarely felt in need of protection, so that couldn't be it. Puzzling over the matter, she finally gave up. She didn't know exactly what she felt, but whatever it was, it was good.

"So? What were you thinking?" He rubbed a lock of her hair between his fingers, tugging gently to get her attention.

Realizing the touch of his hand on her scalp had all but reduced her to purring, she blinked up at his chin, trying to remember. "Oh, about aliens," she said in a soft voice, aware that she was surrounded by true believers and unwilling to hurt them.

He grunted. "Why am I not surprised?"

"To be more specific, I was thinking about my attitude toward the subject."

"Which is?"

She smiled, hearing the amusement in his voice. "I'm a little more tolerant than I was several weeks ago. I was a complete skeptic when we started out."

"And you're not now?"

More amusement, she thought, understanding. "Yeah, I still am, but maybe to a lesser degree. If Aunt Tillie could find a group like this—" she waved her hand, encompassing the seniors around them "—who so completely believes—and it is a *very* intelligent group—who am I to say they're all wrong?"

Shane shrugged, smiling down at her. "I don't know. Who *are* you?"

"Where this is concerned," she muttered, "I'm a journalist. Curious, but with a practical side that demands evidence and proof. Lots of it. I need to see something with my own eyes, something irrefutable, that can't possibly be mistaken for anything else."

"There's nothing wrong with that. In my book, practicality gets you a lot further than gullibility."

"Yeah, but what if—"

"My holy, sainted Aunt Maria!" The strangled whisper came from Jack, and it was a cross between an oath and a prayer. "Red alert, you guys. To the north. Something's coming."

Dave turned in his chair, almost falling. "Where?" he whispered, fumbling for his binoculars.

"There." Jack surged to his feet, pointing. "And it's definitely not a meteor shower."

His voice shaky with excitement, Dave called out to the others. "Remember what we agreed before we left. If we see something unusual, we don't talk, we don't compare notes. We observe and write it down later. Not a word from this point on!"

By this time, they were all on their feet looking up. Christy shivered and touched Shane, wrapping her arm around his waist and tucking her thumb through one of his belt loops, reassured by his nearness, his warmth. Keeping his eyes pinned on the object overhead, he draped his arm around her shoulders, pulling her closer. In the distance, he heard Red calling out to the other men and the sounds of boots scuffling on the bunkhouse porch.

Overhead a huge, dark oval moved slowly through the sky, blocking the glittering stars beyond. It moved so soundlessly they could still hear the crickets chirping around them and the cicadas shrilling a song in the trees.

It glided silently in their direction, coming to a halt directly overhead, settling between them and the moon. The enormous oval body was ebony with the light of the moon turning the rim a rich gold. It was surrounded by the brilliance of the distant stars. Shane tilted his head to listen, but he heard no identifying rumble of an engine.

Breathless, Christy watched. Even without Dave's orders, she couldn't have managed a sound. Nor could she drum up a journalist's shield of objectivity. It was all she could do to stay on her feet and breathe.

Then, after three or four minutes, in the blink of an eye it was gone. The moonlight washed over them again, and the stars above glittered in all their glory. It hadn't flown away, she thought, turning to check the rest of the sky. It had simply...vanished.

"Not a word," Dave called out again. "We'll get some lights on, pass out some paper and have you write your impressions. Estimate the height, size and shape. You know the drill. Put in all the details you can."

Christy scribbled furiously, knowing she was hopeless at calculating the distance and size, hoping the others would be better. Finally, she handed her paper to Dave and turned to Shane, who had finished and was talking quietly with Jim Sturgiss.

Jim shook his head emphatically. "Believe me, this country has no aircraft that big, not even in an experimental phase. That thing looked like it was the size of a football field. I had access to some pretty top-secret stuff while I was in the Air Force, and I haven't been gone that long. There's no way it's ours, and our technology is way ahead of other countries." His brows lifted over steady eyes. "So, my friend, your guess is as good as mine."

Shane reached out, taking Christy's hand, and frowned. "You're cold." He rubbed her hands briskly between his. Looking around, he asked, "Did you bring a jacket?"

She shook her head. "No, but I'll be fine." A quick shiver ran through her, and Shane snagged the blanket at their feet, folded it in half and draped it around her shoulders. Grasping the edges, he tugged until she was pressed against him, snuggling into his heat. She wrapped her arms around his waist and felt the steady beat of his heart against her cheek.

"Want to talk about it?" he murmured.

She shook her head. "Not yet. Give me a minute. I need to come back to earth." She remained where she was, grateful for his rock-solid strength. A few minutes later, she lifted her head and gave him a weak smile. "Wow, it'll be a long time before I do that again."

"Do what?" He tilted her face up, looking for signs of shock.

"Ask for proof or evidence."

Shane's crack of laughter caught Jack's attention.

Walking over, he grinned at the picture they made. Christy, flushing, was fighting her way out of the blanket and Shane leaned against Ruth Ann's RV, still amused.

"What now?"

Shane pointed to Christy. "She thinks she's responsible for the show we just had."

Shaking his head, Jack gave her a commiserating pat on the shoulder. "Sorry, kiddo, you can't be. Tillie's taking all the credit—with all due modesty, of course. After all, didn't her friend, Starman, promise her his friends would drop by? And weren't they going to do it because she was the one—and only— worthy person in the state of Nevada? Maybe in the whole world?"

Christy looked at Jack, stunned. "Aunt Tillie never said that!"

He grinned again. "Not in so many words, but believe me, the message is loud and clear."

"That does it." Christy dropped the blanket and looked around at the delirious seniors, who were now rehashing the event at the top of their lungs. Jack, she noted, was dying to rejoin them. "I need to get away from all this, to walk. But most of all, I need some quiet and a bit of sanity."

"Wait a minute, I'll go with you." Shane grabbed the blanket and followed her, wrapping it around her shoulders again. As they walked in silence toward the barn, away from the others, he reached out and laced his long fingers through hers. After opening the large door and flipping on a few lights, he led her inside, hoping she would be soothed by the warmth and earthy smells of horses and hay.

Letting her go, he sat on a bale of hay, watching with a small smile as the curious horses poked their heads out, ears alert and nickering softly. Now that she was more comfortable around them, he knew she wouldn't be able to resist running her hand down their broad noses, taking comfort from them.

Christy took her time, stopping at one stall then another, murmuring nonsense to the horses, petting them. By the time she worked her way back, she was no closer to understanding what had taken place outside, but she had shed most of the tension that had chilled her so.

Finally, she sat down beside Shane, discarding the blanket behind her. Sighing, she leaned against him, murmuring, "Thank you."

His arm tightened around her waist, pulling her closer, until they felt the warmth of each other from their knees to shoulders. Lifting her chin until his dark gaze held hers, he said tenderly, "It was my pleasure."

His pleasure, she thought, dazed. Two weeks earlier, he had made it abundantly clear that his pleasure was inextricably bound to having her in his huge bed—or anywhere else for that matter. His black eyes had been inflexible, hot and hungry. As far as that went, they still were.

But now, whether he knew it or not, when he looked at her he saw more than just a woman to bed. Oh, he still wanted her, she didn't doubt that for a second; his body told her so every time she came within fifty feet of him. There was something very elemental and earthy about a man who acted like a stallion scenting a mare when he saw the woman he wanted, she thought. And while it might be nerve-racking for the woman involved, it was also damned exciting.

But she needed more than excitement from the man she would let in her life. It had to be mixed with a healthy dose of trust, tenderness, humor, mutual interests and genuine concern. Christy took a deep breath and looked up at Shane, not knowing what she expected to see on his hard face. It definitely wasn't the blend of tenderness and stark hunger that glittered in his dark eyes.

Her earlier chill had passed and she fought the sudden warmth that enveloped her body. She should be getting used to it, she thought in disgust. Every time he looked at her like that, her temperature shot up about ten degrees, her senses felt drugged and her skin was sensitized almost to the point of pain. She was experienced enough to know what sexual response felt like, but she wondered why Shane's reaction to her triggered such upheaval in her body when it had never happened with anyone else. Not even the exes.

The exes had been good men, she thought for the hundredth time, but they hadn't been right for her. And though it was hard to remember when Shane touched her—or even looked at her with that focused hunger—he probably wasn't a better choice. He had a problem with trust. A big one. She didn't know which was more disturbing, that realization or the emotions that jittered through her body when he touched her.

There were times when she wanted to forget her blasted list of priorities and just throw herself at him, letting nature—and Shane—take over. She had a feeling that she wouldn't regret it, at least not for a long, long time. But the day might come when she would, and she couldn't bear the thought of Shane becoming ex number four.

Blinking thoughtfully at their laced fingers, Christy considered the alternative that had been nudging her for the past several days. Shane was not a trusting man; that was a given. But how could a man learn trust from the type of women he had— twice—considered marrying? Obviously, he couldn't.

What he needed in his life was a woman who wanted the best for him, who loved him, who would be as protective of him as a mother with a cub even as she lusted after him. What he needed was some-one like Christy Calhoun in his life. A forever type of woman who was loyal to a fault and believed in till-death-do-us-part happy endings.

A woman like that shouldn't be too hard to find, she thought with a slow grin. Especially when there was one practically sitting on his lap.

Christy drew in a ragged breath, accepting for the first time what she had suspected for several days.

She was in love with Shane McBride.

Chapter Nine

"Where are you off to today?"

At the sound of Shane's voice, Christy looked up from her computer to see him filling the doorway of the RV. His narrow-eyed expression wasn't comforting, but the challenge and disapproval emanating from him wasn't new, she reflected, feeling a familiar flutter of uneasiness in her stomach. Both his controlled anger and her tattered nerves were about a week old.

It made no difference that she knew the cause and he was still groping in the dark; it didn't alter the fact that they were both hurting. The change in her behavior after that brief time in the barn had baffled and infuriated him. She was simply grateful that he chalked up the reversal to skittishness, the vagaries of hormones or some other female thing.

Whatever he thought, it was a hell of a lot better than having him realize she had fallen in love with a man who was as leery of that emotion as a wolf sniffing at a baited trap, she considered grimly.

Anything was better than that.

"Hello, anyone home?" He rapped sharply on the door to bring her wandering thoughts back. "Do you have time for a ride?"

She shook her head, telling herself she was prepared for the quickly masked disappointment in his eyes.

She wasn't.

"Yesterday, when Dave got his new RV and the insurance check, I promised I'd go into Vegas to help him shop. He has to replace everything he brought for the trip."

"He can buy his own damn clothes."

"I promised," she repeated, her voice quiet. Actually, she had volunteered. It was just another way of avoiding Shane, an exercise she had honed to a fine art these past few days. Dave, who was no fool and perfectly able to restock his own RV, had given her a thoughtful look before accepting her enthusiastic offer of help.

"In that case, there's nothing more to say, is there?" The quiet words were a contrast to his sharp gaze. He took one last long look, then turned and closed the door softly behind him.

Less than an hour later, Dave closed the door on her side of the pickup he'd borrowed from Red and, whistling, slipped behind the steering wheel, heading south toward Vegas. "Young lady, it's a damn good thing I'm more than twice your age, otherwise our fine host might be pointing a six-shooter at my belly. Did you see the look he gave me?"

"Don't exaggerate, Professor. You're perfectly safe." Christy smiled at his gleeful expression.

"Actually, it's quite a compliment having a man like that jealous enough to tear off my legs."

Her smile fading, Christy leaned back in the seat, gazing out at the sere land. "I'm sorry you got caught in the middle of this."

His brows rose at her sober tone. "Since I am, may I ask what 'this' is?"

"Strictly between the two of us?" Christy turned to face him.

Holding up a hand as if taking an oath, Dave said, "Scout's honor. No one will ever know, unless Tillie reads my mind. So give, kiddo."

"I guess it's the old story of a man who doesn't want to make a commitment and a woman who can't live without one."

"Christy, if it's any help, most men don't know they want a commitment until the need jumps up and bites them on the nose." He braked for a roadrunner crossing the road and slid a quick look at her. "I'd say Shane's need is getting ready for the big jump."

Fiddling with her seat belt, she shook her head. "I don't think so. He has reasons for not taking the leap."

"At the risk of betraying my sex, I'll tell you that every man does. Most of them are also scared to death." Without giving her a chance to interrupt, he said, "So what are you going to do, chuck him?"

"No." She gazed ahead through the bug-spattered windshield. "Actually, I'm just trying to keep my distance until we leave." Dave was a good listener; he gave her time to marshal her thoughts without interrupting. "While we're gone, Shane and I would both have time to think things over. Then, I thought if we stopped on our way back from Arizona, just to say hello—"

"Yeah, right."

"Shane and I might be able to talk about this…"

"Lust?"

She scowled at him. "Attraction that's…"

"Turning him into a crazed man with murder on his mind?"

"Dave, you're not helping!"

"I'm sorry." He reached out and gave her shoulder a quick squeeze. "But looking at it from a man's point of view, if my woman left for several weeks—"

"I'm not his woman," she muttered.

"I think you are. In fact, I'm surprised Melinda isn't giving odds that Shane is the only one on the ranch who doesn't know it."

Christy blew out her pent-up breath with an aggravated sound. "So, go on," she prompted. "If your woman left—"

"Without a word, I'd be pretty damn sure she wasn't coming back. I'd also figure she didn't care for me enough to stick around. In my younger days, I would have felt sorry for myself and gotten stinking drunk."

"That's a pretty picture," she said politely. "Besides, I wasn't going to leave without saying something."

"Like what?"

"Well," she hesitated, "I don't know. Exactly."

Dave sighed. "Speaking for most of the men in

the world, we're not good at deciphering hints. We almost always come up with the wrong end of the stick, so being vague won't cut it. You've got to be clear."

"How clear?"

"Very. Something like, Shane, I love you. I want to marry you and have your babies. I won't settle for anything less. Think about it. I'm coming back in three weeks and we can talk about it." He shifted his eyes from the road to her horrified face and back again. "Does that pretty much cover it?"

"Well…yeah. I suppose." She looked at him, torn between laughter and stunned disbelief. "I can't say that to him."

"Honey, trust me on this. Don't pretty it up. The more emotions are involved, the less we understand. It'll be even better if you stick to one-syllable words."

"But that's like…hitting him over the head with a club."

He gave her an approving nod. "Now you're talking. We're like mules when it comes to stuff like this. You have to get our attention."

I love you. I want to marry you and have your babies. I love you. I want to marry you and have your babies.

It was dark when Christy walked through Shane's dining room, her nerves jittering as she repeated the words like a mantra. After taking a ragged breath and blowing it out, she stepped into the hallway, rubbing her temples as she headed for his office. The increasing tension of past two days had given her a headache that no amount of aspirins could alleviate.

But she hadn't had to find excuses to avoid him, Christy reflected, stopping a few feet from the door. Shane had taken care of that, disappearing before it was light and returning for a quick dinner, sitting with the men and discussing ranch business. He spent his evenings in his office, attending to paperwork, Hank had explained, shifting his feet uncomfortably.

Yeah, right.

Instead of being uneasy, she should be grateful he hadn't been focusing on her, brushing against her, making her dizzy with his scent, she told herself.

She wasn't.

She should be relieved the rare smiles that lit up his dark eyes weren't aimed at her.

She wasn't.

She didn't want Shane hurt—especially not by her. Damn it, she wanted back the determined, arrogant, difficult, hard-edged man she'd first met, the one who had been convinced he could talk her into his arms and his bed—by the second day, at the latest.

Christy reached out and softly knocked on the open door. "Shane?"

He looked up from the computer, the desk lamp highlighting his hard features, the stubborn cleft chin, straight nose, cool, assessing dark eyes, strong arched brows and thick black hair. Her throat went dry and her heart went crazy.

Polite, he stood and waved to a chair. "Come in."

Sitting, she considered his two, brief words; they

could have come from a courteous stranger for all
the warmth they held.

*I love you. I want to marry you and have your
babies.* "I just wanted to say goodbye," she said
baldly, clasping her hands in her lap to keep them
from reaching for him. "We'll be leaving early, and
you might be gone."

"I know." His voice was calm, as expressionless
as his eyes. "Have a safe trip."

Panic fluttered in Christy's throat. He had closed
down, shut her out, and her courage was fading with
every passing second. *I love you.* "Shane…"

He exhaled sharply. "Yeah?"

"Uh, we'll be back this way in three or four weeks
and I thought, *we* thought," she corrected hastily,
"that we might stop by and…say hello or something."

She thought she would choke on the silence that
followed; it seemed to suck all the oxygen out of the
room. And she wondered how she would ever utter
the words locked so deep in her heart.

"I don't think that's a good idea," Shane said, his
deep voice level. "Once you go, it's better to leave
it that way." He reached out to touch the save button
on the computer, watched the screen flicker and turn
off with a finality that made Christy blink. "I said
my goodbyes to the others earlier this evening," he
said, rising. "I hope you all find what you're looking
for." He met her bewildered gaze for a brief moment, then held out a hand, indicating the door. "Do
you want me to walk you back to the RV?"

Christy stood and blindly made her way to the
doorway. "No. Thank you." *I love you.* She hesi-

tated, stunned by how quickly it had all gone wrong. "Shane, I—"

"What?"

At the impatience in his voice, she stiffened her spine and began walking down the hall away from him. "I'll be just fine." She left him there in the office, going out the back door and down the stairs, her mind repeating the words she had been unable to say: *I love you. I want to marry you and have your babies.*

For the next three weeks Christy did her level best to forget Shane. The fact that her best wasn't good enough was a source of constant irritation and pain.

She drove the RV, following the schedule agreed upon by the seniors, using their method of discussion and consensus as a basis for one of her articles. She soft-pedaled the fact that the discussion was often heated and consensus was arrived at only when they were all exhausted.

They stopped at Ehrenberg where hikers had reported that "things" flew over the mountains. The seniors were particularly interested in the petroglyphs and enigmatic ground markings. Reports of amorphous blue lights—on the ground and in the sky, turning everything blue—drew them to Gila Bend.

Picacho Peak, where years earlier multiple witnesses reported seeing a cigar-shaped craft land, particularly fascinated the seniors. Christy volunteered to take and transcribe notes of the stops so the seniors could snoop without hindrance.

Even though she crammed every hour of her

schedule with work and reading Shane's great-grandmother's diary—which she had found in the RV the night after they left—there were too many idle moments to think. Brood was more like it, she decided, after several sleepless nights spent regretting the tender words she hadn't said to Shane and shaping a few choice phrases that she should have.

Pain and regret eventually turned to simmering anger and impatience. Damn the man! He had ended something that could have been wonderful and precious—and he did it because he was afraid. She could understand the fear, but not the fact that he had made a decision affecting both of them without saying a word to her.

He didn't have the right, she fumed silently. Who *gave* him the right? How would he like it if she just took off without saying a word to him—especially about something— The realization that she had done precisely what she was accusing him of stopped her short for a long moment.

Another flash of temper set her rolling again. Of course she had. Anyone with an ounce of pride would have done the same. After all, hadn't he almost frozen her with his cold courtesy?

You bet he had.

And hadn't he shut off that computer right in her face, symbolically closing her off at the same time?

Absolutely.

Hadn't he, when she suggested returning to the ranch, told her not to bother? Said it wasn't a good idea?

Hell yes!

So why should she be concerned about an impatient, rude and hard man who told her to go away and leave him alone? she fretted, her eyes narrowed on the road leading them to Sedona.

Because he touched her soul in a way that no other man had?

Maybe.

Because he was a man who needed the kind of love she had to share?

Possibly.

Because he left a hole in her heart the size of Grand Canyon?

Absolutely.

And what was she going to do about it? Probably nothing, she admitted. What *could* she do—knock him out, tie him to a rock and *make* him listen? Sure.

"Almost there," Tillie sighed, giving a wiggle of anticipation in the seat next to her, scattering Christy's thoughts. "We've seen so much these past three—almost four—weeks since we left Shane's, but I'm glad we left Sedona for the last."

Christy smiled at her aunt's enthusiasm, wishing she had just a fraction of it.

"You will, dear."

"Will what?"

"Have it."

"It?" Grinning, Christy looked at Tillie and said, "Why is it that I always sound like an echo when I'm around you?"

"Enthusiasm," Tillie said, responding to the first question. "And joy, of course."

Trying to unravel her aunt's comment, Christy turned back to the road. "I will? Have it?"

Tillie nodded. "Indeed you will."

"So when do I get it? I'm due for some."

"I'm not...it isn't... The older woman sighed. "I don't know. But Walter reminded me just last night that neither you nor Shane can change your destiny."

Christy's heart leaped. "Did he, uh, give any clues about the nature of it?" she asked delicately. "Our destiny, I mean."

Tillie shook her head. "No more than usual. Oh, look!" She pointed to a sign ahead, excitement raising her voice a notch. "It's only thirty miles."

Sedona, home of crystals, the harmonic convergence, channeling and vortices, Christy thought, wondering what mysterious elements the seniors would find there. And how much trouble they'd encounter along the way.

"Enhanced energy," Tillie said placidly.

"I beg your pardon?"

"That's what happens in Sedona to a lot of people. I think all the energy in a vortex enhances an individual's energy."

"I've read about the vortices, of course, but how would *you* describe one? In simple terms, please."

"Places of great energy. Not moving or spiraling energy like tornadoes," Tillie explained. "Just wells or springs of energy."

"And they do what?"

"Walter says..."

Christy groaned. "I thought you were going to keep it simple."

Tillie gave her a patient look. "A vortex has energy." Her tone was that of a teacher repeating a lesson to a slow student. "A person has energy. The energy emanating from the vortex intensifies the person's energy, allowing the person to be more of what he or she can be!"

"Oh. Right." Christy rolled her eyes and pressed harder on the gas pedal.

"And that's what we'll find when we climb Bell Rock this afternoon." Tillie sat quietly for a few moments then cleared her throat. "I had a chat with Walter this morning."

Christy tensed at her aunt's tentative comment. "Oh?"

"He seems concerned about you and Shane—the two of you."

"There is no two of us," Christy said, her voice level. "We're two individuals, each going our own way."

"Oh, dear."

"What?"

"I don't think Walter understands that. He kept repeating your names and the same three words over and over."

"I'm going to hate myself for asking," Christy muttered, "but what three words?"

Tillie brightened. "They're *good* words," she promised.

"Aunt Tillie, *what* three words?"

"Love, marriage and babies."

"Boss?" Hank dropped into the chair across from the desk, slid down until he was sitting on his spine and crossed his long legs at the ankles.

Shane looked up from the manila envelope he was holding, his face grim. "Yeah?"

"Red's goin' into town and wondered if you wanted him to pick anything up."

"No." A sudden flash of temper narrowed his eyes, and he dropped the envelope. "And why the hell are you running his errands? He can ask me himself if he wants to know."

"Nobody with any sense is comin' in here to ask you anything," Hank drawled. "There ain't no flies on that boy. You've been about as sociable as an ulcerated tooth this past month."

Shane grunted. "*You're* here."

"Yeah, well probably because you ain't gonna yell at me or tell me to get out. And if I'm lucky, you might even fire me."

Running his hands through his hair, Shane gave a disgusted sigh and leaned back in his chair. "I know. I'm sorry. I've been hell on wheels to get along with."

"Nah. It ain't been that bad." When Shane's brows rose in disbelief, Hank grinned. "It's been worse." Pushing up a bit in the chair. "Old son, I think you need to get away for a while. Why don't you go to Vegas and give the crap tables a dustin'?"

Shane shrugged. "I don't know if I'm in the mood." He wasn't in the mood for anything—except finding Christy and hauling her back to the ranch.

"It's been four weeks now." Hank gave a long, drawn-out sigh. "I bet those RVs will come rollin' in here just so those folks can say hello before they head back home."

"No they won't," Shane said in an even voice. "I told her not to come back."

Hank sat up straight, staring at him. He opened

his mouth, then closed it. Finally, he said mildly, "I know you can be some stubborn, but you ain't never been dumb. Why'd you do it?"

"Because she has a life of her own and she doesn't want to spend it on a ranch." Shane swiveled in his chair to gaze out the window at the rolling green fields, turning his back on his old friend.

"Did you ask her?"

"She told me loud and clear what she wanted. An editor's job in L.A. was high on the list."

"And what were you offering?"

Shane stiffened at the blunt words. "What exactly are you asking me?" His voice was dangerously soft.

"Permanent or not?" Hank asked, not backing down.

"Not."

The chair creaked when Hank got to his feet. "You may not be dumb, boy, but you are a fool. That gal's a keeper, and seems to me, when you find one like that, you don't play games." He left the office, his footsteps louder than usual as he stalked down the hallway.

The heavy silence in the room was finally broken by the loud peal of the telephone. Shane swung around, snagged the receiver and snarled, "Mc-Bride."

"Shane?" The startled voice belonged to Tillie. "Dear boy, you don't sound at all like yourself. Are you all right?"

"Yeah, I'm just dandy."

"Oh, good." Relief colored her words. "I've been worried. Walter, you know. He says something bad—'' She stopped and tried again. "It's outside, whatever it is.''

"Whatever *what* is?''

"The thing that's going to happen. You wouldn't like to stay in the house for a day or so, would you? Walter would feel much better.''

"Tillie, I'll be fine,'' he assured her. "Don't worry.'' He wouldn't ask, he told himself. It was none of his business. Flinging his own advice aside, he said in a casual voice, "By the way, where are you?''

"On our way back to Las Vegas. I'm sorry, but we won't see you this time. Oh, Shane, we had a wonderful time in Sedona. The police sent a helicopter out to Bell Rock to tell us we couldn't have a public meeting up there.'' Indignation sharpened her voice. "We weren't! We simply stopped to meditate, and a number of people joined us. Then I almost fell off, but it was my own fault. I had my eyes closed, drawing in the energy, and I tripped. But Jack and Melinda saved me. I'm very pleased with them.''

Shane blinked. "You are?''

"Oh, yes. There's a fine romance developing there. Just think, they might not have met if it hadn't been for this trip.''

"Tillie, how's Chri—''

"Oh, dear. We're getting ready to leave now. Remember, dear, be careful.''

Chapter Ten

Tillie wouldn't be pleased, Shane thought the next morning as he cleared his desk. He wasn't going to stay in the house. He had finally given in and agreed to leave for a few days.

Actually he'd been forced into it when Hank's pointed suggestions had finally turned into a confrontation. "The herds have to be moved. I know what I'm doin' and so do the men. We don't need you along for the two or three days it'll take us. Hell, the way you've been actin', we don't want you to come—*period.* We're bringin' Hector along to do the cookin', so you might as well take off. That way, you still might have a crew when you come back. And I told Adelaide to take a few days off, so she's gone to her sister's."

Hank was right, he knew. Nothing the men had done in the past four weeks had been good enough for him. He had driven them as hard as he'd pushed himself until Hank had finally gone nose to nose with him.

They had taken off before dawn, and he would leave soon for…hell, he didn't know where. Anywhere as long as it wasn't Vegas. Not while there was a chance that Christy and her gang of seniors were still there. Big as the place was, it would be his luck to run into them. He crammed the large manilla envelope that had arrived the day after Christy left in the top drawer. It was just as well she hadn't seen it, he decided. It had been a crazy idea.

He jammed a bulky white envelope on top of it and tried to shut the drawer, swearing in exasperation when it wouldn't close. Pulling it back out, he studied it, vaguely remembering that Ruth Ann had handed it to him the night before they'd left. He tore it open and upended it on his desk. A map, accompanied by a note and business card, fell out.

He picked up the card first, swiftly reading the name, R.A. Watts, Hydrologist. He gave a long, drawn-out whistle as it slipped through his fingers, falling on top of the map. Ruth Ann, the woman he'd indulgently allowed to wander around dowsing on his land was R. A. Watts, with a doctorate from the Colorado School of Mines. She was also one of the top hydrologists in the country; the one who'd been booked up for several years in advance each time he'd tried to hire her to test his land for water.

Unfolding the map, he saw it was the one of his ranch that she had requested the day after they'd moved up by the house—the one he'd handed out so carelessly that he'd forgotten about it. The arid section of his property had a number of various colored dots marking it.

The note was brief:

Dear Shane,

The enclosed map is my attempt to repay you for your hospitality. Don't be put off by the dowsing; it's always my first step in a project. It has proven to be almost infallible.

The red dots indicate areas I consider to be extremely good possibilities. The green are the next level, followed by the blue. You'll find that we staked the marked areas with appropriate colored flags.

Best of luck,

Ruth Ann

Two hours later, Shane led a sorrel mare out of the barn, his bedroll strapped on behind the saddle. The horse was one he was still training, but it had stamina. Tillie definitely wouldn't be happy, he reflected, touching the folded map in his shirt pocket next to the cellular phone. He was going to check out every one of the staked areas, and if a hundred Joshua trees fell on him in the process, it would just be too damned bad. At least he wouldn't be turning a corner and running into a curvy redhead who had stolen part of his heart—along with his great-grandmother's diary.

Christy closed the diary, murmuring, "And they lived happily ever after."

"Who's that, dear?" Tillie stopped struggling

with the yards of lace she was wrapping around her diminutive body to look curiously at her niece. It had taken her longer than she'd expected to find the proper clothes for spending a day in a casino.

"Shane's great-grandparents."

"Yes, the dear boy came from good stock."

"How do you know?" Christy lifted a strip of lace from the floor and handed it to her aunt, watching as Tillie wrapped it around her narrow waist like a cummerbund.

Tucking the ends under folds of fabric, Tillie made a tsking sound. "Shane makes no secret of where he comes from, and they don't send weak people, let me tell you."

"Nevada?" Christy said blankly.

"I'll bet it started with his great-grandfather, perhaps even earlier," Tillie muttered from beneath several layers of lace. "Maybe they knew, maybe they didn't. But I'll bet that Shane knows, at least subconsciously." Tillie's glowing face emerged between panels of fabric that fell to her waist.

Baffled, Christy gazed at her aunt. "I don't have the foggiest idea what you're talking about."

Shaking her head, Tillie sighed. "What do his shirts say? What does every pocket on every shirt tell you?"

"Oh, no. Aunt Tillie, you aren't saying that you think he's—"

Tillie nodded, her transparent face beaming. "Galaxy is what it says and what it means. Shane McBride came from another world! Isn't it exciting? First Brandy finds a man from outer space and now you."

"Aunt Tillie, it's just the brand name of his shirt. He buys them because they fit comfortably."

"Of course they do."

"It's only a coincidence," Christy said firmly.

Tillie gave her a blissful smile. "There is no such thing as coincidence. Whatever happens is meant to be." Peering into the mirror, she tugged on an errant wisp of lace. "Are you ready? It's almost time to meet Melinda and the others."

The rest of the seniors had gathered in the hotel lobby, where they had checked in after returning their RVs and renting a van. They were eager to hit the blackjack tables. With a month's worth of tutoring from Melinda and Jack, who had learned some of the finer points of gambling while he worked in vice, they were hoping to beat the odds and come away big winners. In the background the clank of coins falling in the metal coin returns of slot machines was a siren call to innocents with well-padded pockets.

Tillie opted for the slot machines. "Blackjack's really no fun when you know what cards are coming up. Besides," she murmured, an avid gleam of determination in her blue eyes, "I'm going to find a way to win on these machines."

"I'll stick with Aunt Tillie." Christy tagged along behind her, as much to keep an eye on her as to check out her system. Tillie zigzagged her way through the maze of slots, stopping occasionally, as if listening to soundless voices.

Eventually, she sat before a machine with bars, bells and fruit. Looking around, she finally pointed Christy to one three seats away. Armed with rolls of quarters, she began dropping in coins, grinning when they began returning to her in larger and larger numbers. Christy, she noted, was having the same luck.

Opal and Skip wandered by and watched for a few minutes. When Tillie looked up inquiringly, Skip shrugged. "We know how to play, but we still didn't win. Thought we'd use our last few bucks on these."

Tillie gazed around before pointing Skip to one machine and Opal to another. Soon, the sound of their winnings was indicated by a regular barrage of coins.

When Claude and Ruth Ann drifted by Tillie silently gestured them to certain machines. Ben, Jim and Dave showed up a few minutes later.

Within an hour, their machines were triggering bells and sirens, notifying the casino employees that larger than usual amounts were being won. A half hour later, their consistent luck had drawn a crowd, including some of the hotel security.

Jack shouldered his way through the crowd, standing behind Tillie. "You're making security nervous," he murmured. "I think it's time to hit the trail, podner."

Tillie nodded, but Jack saw her mind was not on the machine before her. Apparently, once she had proven to her satisfaction that she could pick the winning machines, her interest had waned. She dumped her coins in one of the cardboard cartons provided by the casino and handed it to Jack. Folding the larger bills in one of her many lace pockets, she turned and headed toward the cash counter. The others followed as if they were steel shavings drawn to an enormous magnet. Behind them, there was a mad rush for their machines.

"Onward," Skip said with an exultant laugh. "To the next casino, and to hell with the blackjack tables." Most of them grinned and nodded in agreement, but Tillie seemed lost in thought.

"Tillie," Jack asked gently. "Are you okay?"

She blinked, her blue eyes sharpening as she looked at him. "*I* am," she told him, "but there's something wrong and I'm not quite sure—"

"Aunt Tillie," Christy interrupted, taking her aunt's arm and leading her to a cushioned bench. "Maybe you should sit."

As soon as Tillie's narrow bottom hit the bench, she jumped to her feet. "*Shane.*" Her face paled. "He's...hurt." She turned to Jack. "And alone."

He nodded and briskly turned to the others. "Everyone pack a light bag with things for a couple of days and check out of your rooms. I'll keep my room, so leave the rest of your luggage in there. I'll pack and get the van. Meet me in the parking lot and we'll head out in twenty minutes."

Claude, who owned his RV so he could travel with Keno, nodded. "I'll follow the van. We might need some of my equipment."

Back in their room, Christy pulled on jeans and a T-shirt, threw her things into the suitcase and helped Tillie pack. Fear marched through her body in rhythm with her pounding pulse. "Aunt Tillie, is it...bad?"

Tillie turned to face her. "I don't know. It's not at all clear."

"Maybe you're..."

"Wrong?" The word was soft. When Christy nodded, she shook her head. "No, even though it's blurry, it's quite definite."

Shane opened his eyes, looking directly into the sun. Groaning, he blinked several times, to clear his vision. He was flat on his back, had a head that throbbed almost as much as his right ankle, and was looking up at three hawks circling overhead. Grateful they weren't buzzards, he lay there for a moment doing a quick mental survey of his body. Deciding that everything else was working, he sat up and slid his fingers down his boot to check his ankle. Sprained. Bad. But it could be worse. It could be broken.

He rolled over and pushed up to his knees, ignoring the swimming sensation in his head. Once on his feet, he swayed and looked around for the mare—the mare that had stamina but spooked at the whisper of a breeze. In this case, it had been tumbleweed rolling toward them, and he had been so preoccupied with thoughts of Christy he had let down his guard long enough to be tossed on his butt. And his head, he grimaced, gingerly feeling the lump several inches above his nape.

Swearing, he grimly considered his options. It didn't take him long. The horse was gone—probably heading for home—and he was miles away from both the highway and the ranch. He had no water and a bad ankle. Disgusted with himself and the whole situation, he reached for his pocket and the cellular phone. He could call Hank or one of the men to come get him. They'd never let him forget it, but after what he'd done, he deserved whatever they handed out.

He dug behind the folded map in his pocket, reaching for the phone. When his fingers slid to the bottom of his pocket, he yanked out the map and checked again. Empty. The damn thing was gone. Resting his weight on his left leg, he scanned the area, spotting his sunglasses about six feet away. Beyond that was something dark at the foot of a boulder.

He hopped in that direction, snagging his dark glasses along the way. When he reached the rock, he gazed down grimly. The phone was in two pieces, most of its innards scattered in the hard-packed dirt.

"Well, hell," he muttered, looking back the way he had come. "Looks like I've got one choice left. Walk out."

It wouldn't have been a bad walk if he'd had the use of two good feet, he reflected, but with a bad ankle it was going to be a long haul, so he might as well get moving.

Easier said than done, he thought, coming to a stop in the sparse shade of a Joshua tree a few minutes later. Already breathless and soaked with sweat, he knew he couldn't hop much longer without causing muscle spasms on his left side, and touching his right foot to the ground wasn't something he wanted to do very often. Ignoring the deepening pain in his ankle, he looked around for something he could use for a crutch.

Since there was nothing on the ground, he gave the stumpy Joshua tree a swift appraisal. The crooked limbs weren't long enough for a crutch, he decided, but he might make a cane. Digging into his pocket, he pulled out his knife and started hacking at the rough wood.

Two hours later, using the scraggy limb for support, he was making headway. Not a lot, he reflected, stopping to wrap a bandanna around his head, but some. And that was better than sitting in one place until he passed out and turned into buzzard bait. Making his next goal a boulder about fifty feet ahead, he set his teeth and hobbled forward, his thoughts turning to Christy.

He had done the right thing, he told himself. The big seduction scene had fizzled, but it was his fault. The whole mess was his fault. He should have known what kind of a woman she was the minute he laid eyes on her, but his hormones had gotten in the way. He'd wanted her in his arms and his bed, and to hell with anything else.

But not in his heart.

He'd learned the hard way not to trust or love a woman, and he'd kept that thought in mind when he tried to take her to bed. But he'd realized damn fast that Christy wouldn't share her body with a man she couldn't share her heart and soul with. So he'd battled with himself and lost.

She had enough love in her to embrace the entire world, but he couldn't take from her with nothing to give back. He couldn't hurt her. He couldn't maneuver her into a situation that would leave her in pain.

And, hell, even if he could love, they came from different worlds. It was obvious writing was a big part of her life, and she was determined to climb that ladder in Los Angeles. Besides, she couldn't survive in this isolated place. There would be nothing for her to do out here. Nothing to stimulate her sharp mind, nothing to keep her happy. He halted as a shattering insight hit him: he wanted her happy, even if it meant he never saw her again.

The van pulled in behind Shane's house and Christy jumped out with the others right behind her. Claude's RV came to a stop behind them.

"It's awful quiet," Jack said, after a long look around.

Christy headed for the back porch, calling over her shoulder, "Someone check the barn. I'll see if they signed out on the blackboard in the pantry." Claude turned toward the barn, leaving Keno in the RV, but the others crowded in behind her, staring at the message center.

"They're all out on the range moving cattle," Opal said, reading aloud what they all saw. "Even the cook."

Claude slammed the back door as he came in. "There's no one at the barn, but there is a saddled horse. It's got a bedroll and a water flask on it. It doesn't look good for someone."

"Shane," Tillie told them, her voice definite.

Christy drew in a shaky breath. "Shane is the only one who didn't sign out. How can we find him?"

They all turned to Tillie. Flustered, she shook her head. "I don't know where he is."

"But he's hurt?"

Tillie nodded. "But I don't know how bad. I never know. I just see bits and pieces."

Jack nodded and took her arm in a gentle grip.

"Come on," he soothed, leading her to a kitchen chair. "Sit, close your eyes and think about any other images that you pick up."

Obediently, Tillie sat and closed her eyes. "It's dry around him," she finally said.

"Good," Jack said in encouragement. "That cuts the ranch in two. And I'll bet if he took a horse, he wasn't going any farther. So we'll assume he's around here somewhere."

"Water, lots of water," she added. "But I don't understand how I'd see water if everything is dry."

"Don't try to make sense of it," Jack urged. "Just go on."

"Those stumpy trees that look like crooked old men. And dots, lots of dots."

"Dots?" They all looked at each other with puzzled expressions.

"Dots," she said firmly. "And a folded paper."

Jack's brows rose and he turned to Ruth Ann. "Are you thinking what I'm thinking?"

She nodded. "That he went to check the flagged areas we marked for water? Probably. I think we can concentrate on the northern half, because that's where most of the marks are on the map. The dots," she added, smiling at Tillie.

"I think Keno can lower the odds for us," Claude said in a brisk voice. "Someone go rub down that horse with a towel and bring it to me. Jack, can you saddle some horses? And ride?" At the other man's nod, he said, "Good. I want you to go with me in case Shane's unconscious and we have to lift him. Who else wants to go?"

Ruth Ann stepped forward. "I remember the lay

of the land out there and where we put a lot of the stakes. That might help.''

Christy moved beside her. ''I'm going.''

Claude nodded at Jack. ''A horse for each of us and one for Shane.'' Turning to the others, he said, ''Look for canteens and start filling them with water. As many as you can find.''

Thirty minutes later, the four of them rode out from the ranch, heading north, as Ruth Ann suggested. Keno trotted along beside them. When they were well away from the barn, and the mare Shane had ridden, Claude dismounted, holding the towel with the horse's scent for Keno. After a false start, when Keno found the trail but followed the strongest scent and turned back to the ranch, they headed almost straight north. Keno led the way at a fast lope. Claude broke away from the others until he was beside the large dog.

Several hours later they found Shane.

He was sitting in the shade of a boulder but waved and struggled to his feet when he saw the riders approaching, one well ahead of the others. Standing there, supported by his crude cane, he waited. Claude reached him first, with Christy scant seconds behind. Ruth Ann and Jack slowed their mounts when they realized their help wasn't needed.

Jumping off his horse, Claude grabbed a couple of canteens and strode toward Shane. Christy snagged one of them as she tore by him.

''Are you all right?'' she demanded in a fierce voice, thrusting the canteen at Shane. Without waiting for an answer, she scowled at him, her relief spilling into anger. ''Damn it, why didn't you stay inside, the way Tillie told you to? Drink," she ordered when he opened his mouth to respond, backing away so she wouldn't throw herself at him. He didn't want her, she reminded herself. He'd been very clear about that.

Still silent, Shane raised the canteen and drank with greedy thirst. When it was almost empty, he lowered it, his gaze settling hungrily on Christy's worried face. "How'd you find me?"

Claude answered with a relieved grin, realizing the big man was basically in good condition. "Tillie," he said briefly. "And Keno, the wonder dog."

Shane reached down to pat the dog's head. "Keno, from now on you've got a lifetime supply of beefsteak. I'll send it anywhere you want."

"If he ever wants to take you up on the offer, I'll let you know. Where do you hurt?"

Sweeping off his hat, Shane took the other canteen and upended it over his head, letting the water run over him in a cooling stream. "A bump on my head that's minor and a sprained ankle."

Christy glared at him. "You hurt your head and you're standing out here in the sun?"

"I haven't had much choice," he said mildly, his dark gaze taking in her sudden pallor.

"It probably doesn't matter," she assured him. "Your head's so thick I doubt if you hurt it at all. And walking on a sprained ankle's no big deal." She took a shaky breath. "You're a *lunatic*," she said between gritted teeth. "A stark, raving madman."

"Let me take a look at your head," Claude said, moving behind Shane. "How's your vision? Just one of everything?" When Shane nodded, he motioned to a large, flat rock. "Sit there and let's see if we can get that boot off so I can tape your ankle."

Shane was pulling his boot back on when Ruth Ann and Jack arrived with Milt. He lifted a hand in greeting and reached for the reins. Mounting him, he turned toward the others. "I don't know how to thank you, but I'll try later. Right now, Christy and I have some things to settle, and I'd appreciate it if you'd head back to the ranch and let us follow."

Before they could do more than stare at him, he moved next to Christy. "I probably smell worse than a goat, but I really need you in my arms right now."

Color flooding her cheeks, she simply stared at him. Taking that for a yes, he wrapped his large hands around her waist, lifted and settled her in front of him, almost groaning at the way her bottom settled sweetly against him, her legs brushing his with every breath. Nodding to a grinning Claude, he said, "You can take that one back with you."

With grins to match Claude's, Ruth Ann and Jack nodded and turned their horses around. Claude mounted up and Keno sprang to attention. The two of them caught up with the others and set a brisk pace back to the ranch.

After a long silence, Christy blew at her bangs with an annoyed breath. "Well, that was rude enough."

"Rude be damned," he said, his arm tightening around her. "I had to talk to you."

She stiffened, pulling her back away from his chest. "I think you said everything before I left."

After muttering a soft oath, he said, "I need to see your face while we talk. Bring your knees up."

He shifted back in the saddle and, with easy strength, turned her to face him, settling her against him, her legs straddling his.

Forced to grab his shoulders for support, she gasped when the horse's movement rubbed her against him. "*Shane!* For heaven's sake, this is...embarrassing."

Explosive, Shane thought, maybe dangerous, but not embarrassing. "It's heaven," he said simply. "I want you closer than this, but first we have to talk."

He placed a finger over her parted lips. "You'll get your turn. I was a fool when I sent you away," he said brusquely. "I might as well have cut out my heart and thrown it away. All I could think about was that I'd lost. You were leaving, so I wanted it over with. And I didn't want you coming back for a friendly visit. Everyone on the ranch but me realized I was crazy about you."

"You *wanted* me," she said tartly. "There's a big difference."

"I still do." His sudden grin widened her eyes. "Any way I can get you." His smile faded and his eyes darkened with uncertainty. "I'm hard-headed, and it takes me a long time to realize I'm wrong. I was judging you by what happened with two other women, and I wasn't willing to trust again. But while I was fighting my way back to the ranch today, I knew I was going to find you and tell you what I finally got through my thick head."

"What?" she asked softly.

His arms tightened around her. "That you, my redheaded, self-reliant love, are one of a kind. You have enough love in you to warm the world. If you loved a man—if you loved me—you'd take my shaky trust along with my love and cherish it for the rest of your life.''

He took a deep breath and blew it out. ''So I'm here to tell you, lady, I love you, I trust you and I want to spend the rest of my life with you. So what can I do to make you feel the same way?''

He tossed those last words at her like a challenge, Christy thought, wry amusement curling through the love that had softened her against him. Almost like the night he had asked Ben what it would take to stay on as the cook. But he had come a long way from the man who had protected his heart by telling her not to come back.

''What can I do?'' he demanded again, giving her a fierce look. ''For you? For your career? I don't want this to be a sacrifice, damn it. I want you to be happy.''

''Well, shoot.'' She frowned up at him, aware that his eyes hadn't left her face. ''I was looking forward to telling you how pig-headed you were. That I was furious at you for not seeing what we could have together. That you hurt me, and I don't like to be hurt.'' The muscles in his arms clenched, squeezing her ribs.

''And then I wanted to tell you how much I love you. How much I love the ranch, as long as you come with it. How I discovered I didn't want to be an editor, because I'm a writer—and writers write.

''There's so much to learn out here that I could write about—desert plants, country women, the stars, survival in the desert.'' She threw her arms wide in enthusiasm. ''There's no end to the possibilities. And someday, when I feel ready, I'd like to write a novel.''

Dizzy with relief and loving her excitement, all he could think was, she wouldn't be bored out here. The isolation didn't even faze her. Finally, registering her last statement, his brows rose and he echoed, ''A novel?''

Christy nodded. ''Something about pioneer women,'' she said vaguely, her eyes hazy with thought. ''Based on your great-grandmother's diary.''

Shane hugged her again. ''You can do any damn thing you want as long as you stay here with me.'' His hands slipped to her shoulders and held her back so he could see her face. ''So, Christy Calhoun,'' he said deliberately, ''will you love me, marry me and have my babies?''

The words, an echo of what she had wanted to say to him a month earlier, stunned her. Then, with a smile that nearly blinded him, she threw her arms around his neck. ''Indeed I will, Shane McBride. Indeed I will.''

His kiss, the demanding possession of his lips against hers, tongue inviting hers, the sweetness and passion of it, fogged her mind. She wanted closer, closer, until there was nothing at all between them. Groggy with love and desire, she was vaguely aware of their position on the horse. Each step Milt took created a friction that threatened to set them on fire.

Shane leaned back and shook his head. ''Honey,'' he said hoarsely, ''if we're going to make it back to the ranch, I've got to turn you around.'' His expression was tender, amused and hot with frustration when she sighed with regret.

Tillie's entire party was on the porch waiting for them when they returned. Shane dismounted, reached up for Christy and let her slide down his body. Fire flickered in his eyes at her soft groan. With an arm possessively around her waist, he looked up at the group. "You can congratulate us," he said, smiling broadly. "We're getting married."

With a whoop, the horde descended on them with kisses, hugs and claps on the back. They swept the two of them into the house, with Shane trying not to lean too heavily on Christy as they went up the stairs. Inside, Shane stopped and held up his hand for silence. A shimmer of apprehension slid through him at Tillie's thoughtful expression, but he shrugged it off.

"If you folks will help me set up for a toast to my bride, I'd appreciate it. Crystal glasses are in that chest," he waved toward the corner, "and some champagne's in the pantry. We'll be back in a minute. I have something I want to give Christy."

He limped toward his office, keeping her with him. Ignoring her questioning look, he pressed her down in a chair and dug in the top drawer of his desk and pulled out a large manilla envelope. Perching on the front edge of his desk, his leg brushing against hers, he handed it to her. "My original intention was to give this to you before you left as a remembrance of our time together, but that didn't work out. Now it means a hell of a lot more, it means us—together—through eternity."

With a baffled look, she took it from him and tore

it open. At first, the certificate made no sense to her, then she read it again slowly and lifted her head, her eyes bright with tears. "You bought us a star," she whispered. An incandescent smile broke through the tears. "A star named *Calhoun-McBride*." Jumping up, she launched herself at him, laughing when he caught her. "How did you know?" she demanded. "All my life I've wanted a part of me to be up with the stars, and just like that—" she snapped her fingers "—you did it."

Looking down at her with the half grin that drove her crazy, he said, "This marriage business, how long are you going to make me wait?" He gave her a couple of seconds to think. "Tomorrow? The next day?" he prodded. "I'm not giving you time to back out of *this* engagement. When?"

"Well," she drew out the word and looked at her watch. "How about four hours?"

"What?"

The hot expression flickering in his dark eyes thrilled her, but she took a deep breath and said in a practical voice, "By the time we have champagne with them—" she nodded toward the living room "—shower, change and drive to Vegas, it'll be about that."

Shane grabbed her hand and limped toward the door. "Well, damn, woman, in that case, *move*."

Clutching his gift to her chest, Christy broke away and beat him into the other room. "Aunt Tillie, look!" She brandished the certificate. "He bought me a star."

Tillie's smile was as brilliant as Christy's when she looked at Shane. "What did I tell you?" she murmured, turning to Ruth Ann. "The right man is the one who gives her a piece of the universe."

After Jack and Dave passed out glasses of champagne, Shane drew Christy close. Meeting her soft gaze with his, he said, solemnly, "To my lovely bride." Lifting his head to look at the rest of them, he announced with an exultant grin, "And the wedding will be in several hours."

An hour later, Shane, a cane in one hand and Christy's arm in the other, led her down the stairs where the seniors, in another room, were having a noisy discussion.

"It was energy," Tillie insisted. "I could *feel* the good slot machines. I think something happened to me in Sedona."

"Do you know the odds on something like that?"

"I still say, if you go back too often, security will kick you out."

Shane stopped before opening the door. "We'll have a real wedding," he promised Christy. "As soon as we can pull it together. Whatever you want, wherever you want, okay?"

She nodded. "I'll hold you to that." A thought struck her and she resisted as he tried to nudge her out the door. "Oh, no! Shane, I just thought of something."

"Tell me on the way," he said impatiently.

She shook her head. "No, you'd better hear it now. You may want to change your mind."

Shane gave her a fierce look. "*Nothing* could make me do that. There is *nothing* too bad for us to handle, *nothing* that will put off our marriage, *nothing* that—"

"Tillie thinks we're both from outer space and she'll make our lives miserable," Christy blurted. "Especially when we have a family."

Astounded, Shane looked at her. Whatever dragon he'd been prepared to fight, whatever obstacle he'd considered in that fleeting moment, it hadn't been that. Tillie calling him all hours of the day and night was one thing, but believing they were E.T.s was enough to make a man think.

For a couple of seconds.

"Hell," he said gamely. "I'm tough. I can handle it. Besides, if that's the case, we're a perfect match." His hand tightened on hers as they crept down the porch stairs away from the crowd. "As long as I have you, I can handle anything."

Epilogue

A month later, on a sunny June afternoon, Shane stood at the bottom of the porch stairs waiting for Christy. Behind him were rows of chairs filled with family and friends. At the end of the center row was a flower-bedecked arch where the minister stood.

This was the day he had promised her, and it was exactly where she wanted it—at the ranch. Tillie and her caravan buddies and Christy's large extended family on her side. Adelaide and the men sat in the front row on his side. Hank was duded up in a tux, grinning from ear to ear, proud to be his best man. Adelaide had worked herself into a frenzy of cleaning, polishing and hounding caterers. And the guests had been ordered to dress casually for the barbecue and dance that followed the ceremony.

Christy insisted that Shane meet her at the stairs, that her father join them behind the seated guests and the three of them walk down the wide aisle together.

The door opened quietly and she stepped out, framed against the pale, yellow house. Her dress, which she hadn't allowed him to see, was sleeveless with a slim skirt and a low, square neck. A short veil was tossed back over her glorious hair, and she held a bouquet of pink roses with green leaves and baby's breath. Her gaze met his, and Shane knew it was a picture he would carry in his heart until the moment he died.

She came down the stairs in an eager rush, grasping the hand he held out to her. "Shane," she whispered urgently, "Tillie just told me the whole gang is coming back in a couple of months. Since they never could identify that thing in the sky, they want another shot at it. Will they bother you too much?"

Shane's shout of laughter startled the guests, and they turned, smiling when they saw the groom giving the bride a long, leisurely kiss.

Lifting his head, he smiled down at her. "If I can deal with Tillie thinking we're aliens, I can handle anything. *We* can handle anything."

He backed up an inch or two, removed a smudge of her lipstick with his thumb and said huskily, "Come on, sweetheart, let's go get married."

* * * * *

Soldiers of Fortune...prisoners of love.

Back by popular demand, international bestselling author **Diana Palmer**'s *daring and dynamic* Soldiers of Fortune *return!*

Don't miss these unforgettable romantic classics in our wonderful 3-in-1 keepsake collection. Available in April 2000.*

And look for a **brand-new** *Soldiers of Fortune* tale in May. Silhouette Romance presents the next book in this riveting series:

MERCENARY'S WOMAN

(SR #1444)

She was in danger and he fought to protect her. But sweet-natured Sally Johnson dreamed of spending forever in Ebenezer Scott's powerful embrace. Would she walk down the aisle as this tender mercenary's bride?

Then in January 2001, look for THE WINTER SOLDIER in Silhouette Desire!

Available at your favorite retail outlet.
*Also available on audio from Brilliance.

Silhouette®
Where love comes alive™

If you enjoyed what you just read,
then we've got an offer you can't resist!

Take 2 bestselling love stories FREE!

Plus get a FREE surprise gift!

THE
FORTUNES
OF TEXAS

Membership in this family has its privileges…and its price. But what a fortune can't buy, a true-bred Texas love is sure to bring!

On sale in June…

Wedlocked?!
by
PAMELA TOTH

Once, steely attorney Cole Cassidy had been forced to give up the only woman he'd ever loved. Now Annie Jones was his last hope; he desperately needed her to play his beloved wife. And Cole vowed this undercover bride would be his for real…wedlocked in desire forever!

THE FORTUNES OF TEXAS continues with
HIRED BRIDE
by Jackie Merritt, on sale in July.

Available at your favorite retail outlet.

Where love comes alive™

Look Who's Celebrating Our 20th Anniversary:

"Happy 20th birthday, Silhouette. You made the writing dream of hundreds of women a reality. You enabled us to give [women] the stories [they] wanted to read and helped us teach [them] about the power of love."

—*New York Times* bestselling author
Debbie Macomber

"I wish you continued success, Silhouette Books.... Thank you for giving me a chance to do what I love best in all the world."

—International bestselling author
Diana Palmer

"A visit to Silhouette is a guaranteed happy ending, a chance to touch magic for a little while.... It refreshes and revitalizes and makes us feel better.... I hope Silhouette goes on forever."

—Award-winning bestselling author
Marie Ferrarella

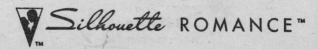

Harlequin is having a *Heatwave*

Featuring *New York Times* Bestselling authors

LINDA LAEL MILLER
BARBARA DELINSKY
TESS GERRITSEN

Watch for this incredible trade paperback collection on sale in May 2000.

Available at your favorite retail outlet.

HARLEQUIN®
Makes any time special ™

Visit us at www.eHarlequin.com

PHEAT

VIRGIN BRIDES

**Join
Silhouette Romance
as the New Year brings new
virgin brides down the aisle!**

On Sale December 1999
THE BRIDAL BARGAIN
by Stella Bagwell (SR #1414)

On Sale February 2000
WAITING FOR THE WEDDING
by Carla Cassidy (SR #1426)

On Sale April 2000
HIS WILD YOUNG BRIDE
by Donna Clayton (SR #1441)

Watch for more **Virgin Brides** stories from
your favorite authors later in 2000!

VIRGIN BRIDES
only from

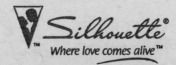

Silhouette®
Where love comes alive™

Available at your favorite retail outlet.

Visit us at www.romance.net

SRVB00